# To the Nimbelum and back
## The tale of a group of winged Space Cadets

By

Alan Johns

MAPLE
PUBLISHERS

To the Nimbelum and back The tale of a group of winged Space Cadets

Author: Alan Johns

Copyright © 2025 Alan Johns

The author asserts the moral right to be identified as the author of this work.

The right of Alan Johns to be identified as author of this work has been asserted by the author in accordance with section 77 and 78 of the Copyright, Designs and Patents Act 1988.

First Published in 2025

ISBN 978-1-83538-657-6 (Paperback)
       978-1-83538-658-3 (Hardback)
       978-1-83538-659-0 (E-Book)

Cover Design and Book Layout by:
       White Magic Studios
       www.whitemagicstudios.co.uk

Published by:
       Maple Publishers
       Fairbourne Drive, Atterbury,
       Milton Keynes,
       MK10 9RG, UK
       www.maplepublishers.com

A CIP catalogue record for this title is available from the British Library.

All rights reserved. No part of this book may be reproduced or translated in any form or by any means, electronic or mechanical, including photocopying, recording or by any information storage and retrieval system without written permission from the author.

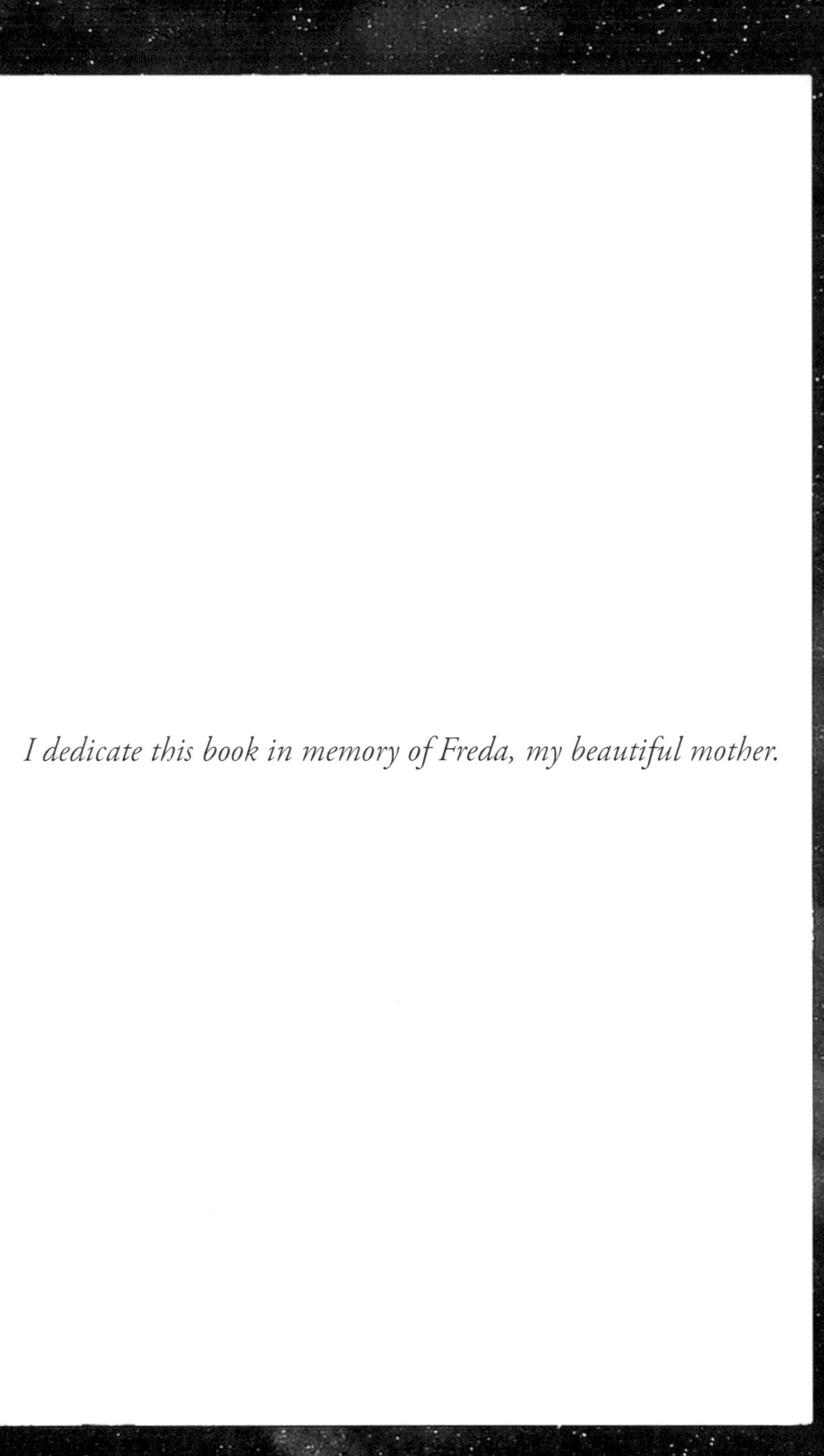

*I dedicate this book in memory of Freda, my beautiful mother.*

It was 07.00 on a beautiful, crisp, very misty, autumn morning. The Emperor Galen had woken early. Galen was a large, muscular butterfly. He was a very dark shade of black with bright red metallic trimmings all around his well- groomed coat. He lived at the top of a cluster of giant oak trees and had just finished his morning exercise, swooping and gliding a long way beneath where his lordly retreat lay.

It was very still at that time of the morning, but Galen had called a meeting to address an issue of great importance.

Even though all butterflies have different personalities, characters, mannerisms and habits, some good and some bad and a bit distasteful, they all possess warm and endearing hearts, little ticking nougats of goodness and warmth toward their fellow wings. They are all connected to each other and know where each one is. This is because a mere flutter of their multi-coloured wings emits an invisible beam of light and creates a small vibration which informs them of where they are and what they are up to. These beams of light are also used to give a sense of direction and thus to minimise direct collision with each other. The source of this great energy belongs to the supreme head of the butterfly population. It is she who possesses such energy as is needed to interweave and interlink the entire butterfly species on earth. Her name is Tindorella and she exists billions of light years away in a space segment called the Nimbellum.

Just recently however, over a period of a few months, reports had been received from around the world, within the butterfly fraternity, that an increasing number of brethren had been either losing their way or had been unable to communicate using the beam of light and vibration method and had subsequently been bumping into hedgerows, trees and all manner of vegetation and undergrowth. A great many of them had damaged their delicate wings and had been grounded. The situation had become so serious that it had come to the Emperor Galen's attention, and it was this that had prompted him to call an important meeting. The meeting was to take place not far from where he lived, in a large opening, surrounded by tall cedar trees interspersed with fallen branches, the result of a severe gale which had occurred several weeks ago. The opening was approximately fifty yards long and twenty five yards wide and Galen had recruited a team of thirty helpers, mostly beetles and spiders, to transform this space into a suitably welcoming, fine cut grass canopy, for the various species of butterfly to land on when they eventually arrived from all directions in what was sure to be a fantastic kaleidoscope of colour and clamour.

The beetles had systematically chomped their way up and down the length and breadth of the opening, devouring all the grass they could eat, with the result that the opening resembled a human bowling green, very finely  cut and ideal for the landing site that awaited the expected audience.

The spiders, for their part, had spun a series of differently coloured webs, commencing from the centre of the opening as fine threads and radiating to the outer edges by which time, the width of each thread was no less than two yards. There were eleven spiders in total, and each spun a different coloured web. They consisted of orange, yellow, green, red, purple, white, blue, pink, black, brown and crimson.

Galen had received posted replies from all invitations sent and it was confirmed that eleven butterfly families would be honoured to attend his important meeting. Each of these families had a favourite colour or were very attracted to one particular colour and so, as a mark of respect and as a welcoming gesture, Galen had employed the spiders to spin all their favourite colours. Galen had also constructed eleven large containers made of redwood bark which he intended to fill with each respective family's favourite food. Make no mistake, butterflies are very fussy eaters and have been known to travel mile after mile in search of their own favourite delicacy. Galen wanted them to feel comfortable at home and at ease before he started his lecture on the utmost important subject. He enlisted the help of a few of his friends to go and collect the required foodstuffs. There were four helpers in total. A great big white bunny rabbit called Toadstool. Toadstool was a very strong albino bunny and had known Galen for a number of years. Secondly, Galen recruited Pointer and Bluntedge, a couple of very lively bright red ladybirds with black markings. They were adept at spotting their target a mile off and had an impressive track record of following instructions down to the finest detail.

Next there was Goldylocks, a golden, black eyed and very sprightly hamster who was always busy stuffing her cheeks full of bits of apple, nuts, raisins and sweetcorn whenever she could find any. She was a burrower and had great respect for Galen. Once upon a time, not long ago, Galen had saved Goldylocks from a gruesome ending at the hands of a large dragonfly who was attempting to suck the blood out of the poor hamster. Galen swooped down and made a very loud clicking, flick, flick, flicking of his wings which had frightened the dragonfly off. Goldylocks was forever in his debt.

The fourth helper that Galen recruited was a dear, sweet cat called Dusty, a black and white tabby with eyes like a hawk and claws like an eagle. Galen had rescued Dusty from a couple of near fatal incidents, one involving a very large spider and the other from a certain trampling by a human rambler. Galen had attacked and eaten the spider and had distracted the rambler by flying across his path at great speed and upsetting his balance. Galen trusted Dusty totally to deliver the required food into the awaiting containers.

The first to arrive at the pre-arranged location, a patch of lawn next to a summerhouse at the bottom of a very long garden, was Goldylocks, who had arrived in a bright blue motorised hamster wheel. She seemed a bit annoyed that she was the first to arrive. "Oh no! Am I the first here?" she moaned.

She didn't have long to wait for company because a rustle in the damp undergrowth about ten yards away, signalled the arrival of Toadstool, hopping and skipping with effortless enthusiasm and energy.

"Hello there Goldylocks, I have not seen you for ages. How are you dear fellow?"

"Hello Toadstool, yes, I am fine thank you. You look well. Galen has called an important meeting, but I don't have a clue what it's about, do you?"

"No but it must be important because he has summoned the main families and has recruited us to collect the food for all concerned", said Toadstool with an unmistakable air of pride at having been chosen for the task. Just at that moment Pointer and Bluntedge, the lively ladybirds flew in and landed on the windowsill of the summerhouse. Chattering and giggling to each other, they seemed oblivious to the company that had already arrived. They did, however, know exactly what company they were in and were just about to greet and introduce themselves when there was a great woosh, woosh, woosh, click, click, clicking noise, accompanied by a powerful gust of wind coming from high above them. A fantastic multicoloured spectacle came rushing through the elm trees and they could see Galen who was hovering about them and descending

very slowly. When he was barely six feet from the ground he stopped, hovering in mid-flight to address his friends.

"Good afternoon my dear friends, I notice that there is someone missing, where is Dusty?"

Just at that precise moment, right on cue, a rustling sound could be heard in the long grass, just behind the summerhouse. Moments later, to the left of the wooden hut strolled in Dusty. He was impeccably turned out, his black and white coat clean and groomed to perfection.

"Good day everybody, I am sorry that I am a bit late. Oh! Hello Galen, I didn't see you up there, how are you my dearest friend?"

"I am fine, thanks Dusty and am glad that you could make it", said Galen with a very pleased expression, happy in the knowledge that his friends had showed up.

Galen began, "I have called you all here today because, as you know, I have summoned the butterfly families to a meeting. I have something to say that is of the utmost importance for the continuing survival of the butterfly species around the world. I cannot say any more than that at this stage. What I would like you to do, is to go deep into the woodland and the forest, following the course of the rivers Avondale and Wanderbridge if necessary and to procure the ideal food for each of the eleven families who are to attend. When you have found them, please bring them to where the meeting is to take place. I have named the meeting place Tindorella's Beacon, and it lies due southeast of Cedar Valley, about ten miles from here. There you will find eleven containers, each one positioned at the end of a differently coloured thread of a spider's web. Each family has a favourite colour, you understand. I would like you to deposit the correct food into the correctly coloured container. Is that clear and does anybody have any questions?" said Galen.

You could sense the buzz of excitement amongst the small gathering, everyone was very still and absorbing what Galen had just said. Just as Galen was about to announce the end of the meeting and to bid them fair speed, Toadstool, with a ruffle of his ears and a twitch of his nose said, "Would it be best to work together or to follow our own individual paths and meet up at an agreed time?"

"That's entirely up to you Toadstool, but in my opinion, it would probably be more productive, and you would cover more ground if you hunted and foraged as individuals" replied Galen.

"Excuse us for interrupting but how long do we have to do the job?" exclaimed Pointer and Bluntedge, chuckling and giggling and speaking exactly in unison.

Galen replied, "I have arranged the meeting for Sunday in the forty second segment of the autumnal lunar cycle at 08.00 hours. If your task can be completed before the fortieth segment, I would be most grateful and very happy. Until we meet again, I bid you goodbye", and Galen, accompanied by a great gust of wind, soared through the early evening sky and was gone.

Goldylocks, Toadstool, Dusty, Pointer and Bluntedge talked among themselves for a full two hours after Galen's departure. They agreed, disagreed, contemplated routes and journeys and arranged timetables, when to meet, what to take, what to eat for nourishment and sustenance and almost everything else that you could think of. They did eventually come up with a plan, an itinerary with which to get the job done.

Come the fortieth segment of the autumnal lunar cycle, the deadline that Galen had set, the task had been completed and the large opening, surrounded by tall cedar trees interspersed with fallen branches, called Tindorella's Beacon was laid out as follows. You may recall eleven differently coloured spider's threads, at the end of each one was positioned a container made of redwood bark. The container at the end of the orange thread was stuffed full of lady smock and wet cabbage, the favourite food of the Orange Tip family. The yellow thread was the favoured colour of the Skipper family and wild strawberry had been provided for them. The green thread favoured the Heath family, and their container had been filled with brambles. The colour red was the sole preserve of who else but the beautiful Red Admiral and his wife and honeysuckle, which they loved, had been provided for them. The purple thread attracted the Burgundy family, and they had been provided with cowslip and primrose. White was strongly favoured by not surprisingly; the White family and their favourite mustard oil was deposited in their container. The Blue family preferred sky blue and wild thyme had been provided. Pink, a very unusual and distinctive colour in butterfly society was unique in attracting the Fritillary clan,

their favourite food consisting of thistle and bramble. The black spider's thread, a very dark and forbidding shade of black, was the favourite of the Brimstone family. Its preferred delicacy was Buckthorn. Brown was the favoured colour of the Tortoiseshell family who adored buddleia and stinging nettle. There were ample portions of this supplied for them. The last-coloured thread crimson was the favourite of the Hairstreak family, and their container positioned at the end of the thread had been filled with acorn cups and oak buds. The scene was set for the gathering to commence.

As the five helpers stood on a raised bank, looking over the ground and at what they had achieved, a sudden rustle high up in the trees diverted their attention. The disturbance grew louder, leaves fell to the ground and six beautiful tortoiseshell butterflies swooped down, circled the beacon several times and eventually landed on the food which had been provided for them, buddleia and stinging nettle. No sooner had they settled, a much louder crash, bang, wallop, like a crack of thunder echoed around the opening. This was followed by an array of dazzling hues and colours emanating from at least two different directions. Three of the invited families had arrived at the same time, the orange tips, the skippers and the burgundy families. As they broke through the trees and descended onto their respective foods one could make out their differing flight patterns. The orange tip with its slow, timid flight, but very distinctive with its orange tips on each wing. The skippers and their skipping and dancing movements and the powerful, warrior like burgundies who although one of the smaller types, move with an air of authority. It was they who reached their food first. Twenty-four individuals had arrived, and forty-two were yet to make an appearance. Within the next twenty-four hours the other seven families had arrived. It was now 18.00 hours, the sun was warm and glowing, a gentle blue sky stretched as far as the eye could see and Tindorella's Beacon was a mass of butterfly life. There was a din of general chattering, and all sixty- six individuals were awaiting the arrival of the Emperor Galen. As the clamour and buzz died down, one could feel the expectant anticipation and excitement among the audience while waiting for the host to arrive and sure enough, within a few minutes, Galen appeared from behind a giant, distinctly gnarled tree. His appearance prompted an impressive, thunderous sound of winged applause, a sound produced by a frantic clapping together of each individual pair of wings, a sound not unlike that produced by a thousand castanets.

"Welcome to you all and thank you for coming" shouted Galen as the applause eventually died down. "I have called you to this meeting today because I have been informed that throughout our population there have been reports of individuals losing their way, bumping into obstacles such as hedgerows, bushes and trees. Individuals have also been weakening for no reason whilst in flight and even dying!".

This last word produced many cries and moans from among the stunned audience and a great many looked visibly shaken.

"This has been caused by, and I have it on good authority, that our great mother Tindorella, has developed a serious virus which is both preventing and impeding her supreme ability to co-ordinate and control our movements back here on earth. Our colleagues the Dragonflies, who as you know, patrol the distant segment of space called the Nimbellum where our great mother resides, have reported irregular and highly unusual cloud fluctuations, consistent with an entity or body which is sneezing quite violently and shedding millions of its lightning cells. This is in turn, making her weak and unable to perform her essential functions for our benefit back here on earth. The dragonflies carried out reconnaissance flights on a grid pattern all over the Nimbellum and did indeed locate a very tired, pale and sick looking Tindorella. When they tried to communicate with her, she spoke faintly by illuminating a few million fairy lights but even as she tried to speak, huge numbers of cells were flying off her into darkest space and were forming vapours many millions of light years away. They informed me that she appeared to be slowly disintegrating and getting weaker by the minute".

A brief description of Tindorella's birth, childhood and glorious adult life is necessary at this point in our story to give the reader a small glimpse of her majesty and great importance to the butterfly population in general.

Tindorella was born in the constellation of Scorpius and started out as a little star. She was at this time, one of the brightest little stars in the galaxy. Her mother Angelina was a large, beautiful star who nurtured Tindorella and looked after her, keeping her away and protecting her from free floating gaseous globules which would have attacked and killed her. As Angelina aged (as we all do of course), she started to shrink and fade and eventually turned into what is commonly called a white dwarf, that is, just gas and dust. Tindorella meanwhile, grew through childhood into a great star, many hundreds of miles wide. She grew multicoloured and was very beautiful. The fast, surrounding stellar wind inflated two enormous bubbles, one on either side of her, these became her wings and with these wings, she was able to fly many millions of miles throughout the cosmos growing in strength and beauty and eventually commanding attention from the whole butterfly population on earth. She was a giant who loved and cherished her butterfly children and they in turn, would do anything for her. Tindorella naturally attracted many potential male suitors including a few ugly looking galactic containers, ghostly wanderers, dirty snowballs of frozen gas and dust, but she wasn't interested in any of them. She was committed and dedicated to her butterfly family. It was now the turn of her butterfly family to assist her in her moment of need and to this end Galen addressed his audience.

"I have a plan, a bold and ambitious rescue plan", announced Galen. "We shall go to her assistance. I have drawn up plans to construct a spaceship capable of flying to the outer reaches of the solar system and onto the distant quadrants of space, to reach our loving mother and to give her the help she needs, to restore her back to her radiant self'.

There was a tremendous round of applause, and a member of the Burgundy family suddenly shouted out "But what is ailing Tindorella, Emperor Galen?"

Galen replied, "At this moment in time we are uncertain as to the cause but as we speak, the Dragonflies are attempting to find out more and we should know in due course. In the meantime, I have selected an elite crew of the best, most steely nerved and highly decorated of our brethren for this very daring and crucial rescue mission". There were gasps and highly pitched buzzing noises coming from the excited audience as Galen continued, "I have selected Groundhog as the spaceship commander".

Towards the middle of the great congregation sat Groundhog, a large, muscular fellow. He was the Red Admiral and was in attendance with his wife Barchetta. He had a vivid red band right across his velvet black body, and he looked up and flapped to attention when his name was mentioned.

"Do you accept this great honour of leading the rescue mission?" shouted Galen.

"It would be an honour," replied Groundhog.

Red Admiral Groundhog was a seasoned campaigner who had fought in both major battles against the birds and the frogs.

Galen continued, "I have selected as second in command, Shunter from the Blue family."

Shunter made himself known, situated as he was at the back of the audience, by emitting a rather loud thrashing together of his wings. "I am very honoured and privileged to have been chosen for the challenge," replied Shunter rather excitedly. Shunter was an intense, metallic turquoise colour and was a valuable addition to any space rescue mission because of his experience as a roving, intergalactic specialist engineer.

"Apart from Groundhog and Shunter, there will be a crew of ten, consisting of five males and five females" continued Galen. "The five males are Roebuck, Deadwing, Firefly and the brothers Thunderfly and Thunderbox. The five females are Hazelwing, Twiglet, Bramdean, Echoes and Crystal Tip. Would all the named crew members please come up to the front and stand here with me?"

It took about five minutes for everybody to arrive next to Galen.

"These of your brethren my friends, are the individuals who are going to our mother in her hour of need and are hopefully going to restore her back to her natural health and glory," said Galen, pointing with his outstretched wing to the crew before him. A huge round of applause and a deafening sound of cheering and shouting greeted Galen's announcement. It lasted for a good fifteen minutes before Galen rose up about ten feet from the ground with his big, black wings outstretched, in order to quieten the congregation once more because he had something else to say that was very important, that of the construction of the spaceship and the source of the enormous power needed for it to reach its destination. As he rose, the audience quietened.

"The vehicle that is going to take the crew to Tindorella has been named Sunjammer, so called because of its almost total reliance on the sun for power to transport it across the cosmos. It is approximately ten feet high and is constructed of acorn cups, bamboo canes and sunflowers. It has a fishbowl cabin that is almost totally covered in sunflowers. It is these sunflowers which will attract the sun and propel the ship toward the stars. A giant, woven swatch of cobwebs and a mass of butterfly wings will act as sails. To obtain lift off and to propel it from earth, I have once again enlisted the help of our great friends and allies, the spiders. They are in the process of constructing a super strong web which will act as a catapult to hurtle Sunjammer beyond our orbit and out towards the far solar system. From that point on, the sun shall be the only source of power."

The butterfly audience gasped in amazement as they tried to take in what was being said.

'Now you may be asking yourselves, how are we going to restore Tindorella to her full strength, vitality and beauty," continued Galen. "I shall disclose all, my dearest companions. The crew of Sunjammer are to take with them six cylindrical, golden caskets. These will measure six inches in diameter and ten inches in length and each will contain multicoloured angel dust particles. These particles are to be released next to Tindorella, to enable her to breath them in and for her to generally bathe in them, in the hope that she is fully restored to health".

Galen then announced that he had finished everything that he had wanted to say and that the meeting was now adjourned. With that announcement, the audience began to disperse, and a mass of colours could be seen flying in all directions, through the trees, over the trees and even under the trees. After about forty minutes, the only butterflies left were Galen and the crew of Sunjammer.

"Does anybody have any questions with regard to the mission?" asked Galen.

"Yes sir, how long do you think it will take to reach Tindorella and will she have been informed of the plan to assist her?" said Groundhog.

"Please be prepared for a long, dangerous and very uncertain mission, Groundhog" exclaimed Galen. "I would estimate that you would require a time span of up to six months, from the moment you leave Earth until you reach your final destination at the heart of the Nimbellum. You will have to navigate our Solar System with its many unpredictable Planet atmospheres and associated wind and cloud currents, and you will also have to traverse the outer galaxy, which is shaped like a giant Catherine wheel. As to your other question of Tindorella having been informed, I can assure you that she has been approached by the dragonflies, but they tell me that she is so sick and weak that they don't believe she comprehended what was being said to her. She did, however, seem pleased and she gave them a momentary sparkle of her remaining fairy lights which deeply moved the dragonflies. Are there any more questions?"

After a short silence the meeting was adjourned and after our intrepid crew had conducted a short conversation among themselves, they bade farewell and thanked Galen for everything that he had done. Off they flew in a very rigid, orderly formation through the trees. Galen hovered in silence; his mission accomplished. He was very pleased with himself, the meeting had gone well, he had selected his crew, and he hoped against hope that the mission would be successful and that Tindorella would shine brightly once more. With a sudden loud beating of his beautiful wings, Galen turned and flew from whence he had come, through the tall cedar trees to the giant oak that was his home.

The crew of Sunjammer had, by this time (a few hours had passed) reached the training complex that was to be their home for the next few months. It was a long, deserted thirteenth century human monastery nestled high up in the misty mountains in the land called Silverdell. They had everything here that they needed. An ample supply of food, plenty of fresh water from the mountains, secure comfortable accommodation in the form of lichens and a beautiful red and scarlet moss creeper which had grown upon the sides of the ruined remains of the monastic buildings. So, for the next three months, they trained hard. After this intensive training period they were super fit. Bodies packed with muscle and wings bristling with health and colour. Meanwhile, about twenty kilometres away, in a dormant volcanic crater, the spiders had been very busy assembling the spacecraft. The craft itself was an amazing spectacle, and it had all the features and accessories necessary, to handle a mission such as this. The spiders had been working on it for about six months and during this time, they had constructed between them, a super strong, indestructible web, the very web that was to catapult Sunjammer into the deep reaches of space and towards Tindorella. Finally, everything was ready. The crew were ready, and the only thing left was for everybody to assemble at the allotted time, at the launch site. The location chosen was a distant, bitterly cold ice mountain named Erebus, somewhere in Antarctica.

Our super fit crew travelled from Silverdell to Mount Erebus in a perfect convoy and made it in two weeks.

The dragonflies were again instrumental in transporting the spacecraft, together with the catapult web, which had been rolled up and placed in a casket, to the launch site. This took them three weeks and Sunjammer was finally lowered very carefully, onto Erebus's volcanic lip, at its very summit. Everybody was very excited and not a little nervous. The next stage was to wait for the correct weather conditions to prevail.

You see, low, slow-moving clouds were a key feature here. As the dragonflies were putting the finishing touches to the spaceship and attaching the catapult web to its couplings, Cristal Tip and Roebuck, the climate and botanical experts were scouring the sky, looking for a suitable large, fluffy cloud. After about three hours, Roebuck screamed "Here's one, here's one, let's be quick".

The whole operation was over in a flash. The crew, complete with spacecraft and the three strongest dragonflies boarded a huge white fluffy cloud. The dragonflies proceeded to unfurl the tough spiders web and when fully stretched it measured fifty feet in length. The cloud would take them to a wind vortex, a form of whirlwind, and then whoosh, the team would release the web and Sunjammer and its crew would be up and away. It took a few days of travelling on the cloud, where the company confronted storms, gales, snowfall, hailstones and strong wind currents before they finally encountered a supersonic tube or wind vortex. At this point, the three dragonflies released the web and Sunjammer was propelled beyond the Earth and into space. The sheer power and force of the spiders' web took them behind the moon and as they hurtled at colossal speed away from the Earth's atmosphere, they looked on in amazement at the Earth and a full moon in almost total alignment with one another.

It was time to check all controls and functions and to contact mission control.

"Hello mission control, this is Bramdean (radio operator) calling from Sunjammer, do you read me? Over."

"Greetings Bramdean, this is mission control, we read you loud and clear. Please relay your co-ordinates.  Over"

"Co-ordinates are 45.150 west and 165.251 south east heading away from the moon and toward Mars. Over".

"Bramdean, this is mission control, co-ordinates are spot on. We have Sunjammer on our screens and she is looking good. Butterfly wings are all intact. Could Firefly (the Pilot) please centre the vanes on the corners of the sails and activate the lasers? Over".

"Successful movement completed" responded Firefly.

"Can you please check that all sunflowers surrounding the cabin are intact and fully operational? Over."

After a short while came the reply, "Everything in place and fully functional"

"Received. Firefly will contact you later, over and out".

After about an hour, Groundhog called a meeting in the conference room and of course, everyone attended.

"I need to check that all systems are fully functional and that everybody is aware of the objectives of our mission" announced Groundhog.

Shunter (Engineer) "Everything okay, sir".

Bramdean (Radio Operator) "Everything perfect sir"

Echoes (Sonar}" Screens fully operational sir".

Deadwing (Chief Gunner)" Guns and plenty of ammunition at the ready Commander".

Thunderfly and Thunderbox (Navigators) "All ready and good to go sir".

Firefly (Pilot) "Have just been through controls check with mission control and all is okay sir?"

"Very good", announced Groundhog,"now back to your stations but not before some refreshment and an hour's relaxation".

As the crew talked among themselves and made their way to the dining area and relaxation lounge, Sunjammer was cruising at great speed toward the rings of Saturn. The temperature outside was extremely cold but the rings seen from a distance, were stunningly beautiful. They are made up of particles, about the

size of bricks and are coated with frozen gas. These particles are positioned in a very unique way by frozen ringlets which interact with Saturn's many moons, about fifty-six in all, and it is this interaction that shaped the rings of Saturn. The rings are about 170,000 miles apart from one another.

As Sunjammer passed between the rings and flew past Enceladus, Saturn's brightest moon, (its covered in ice and reflects lots of light) the crew had returned to their stations and were content and happy with the fact that all was running smoothly.

Suddenly, there was a blinding flash and Sunjammer jerked violently toward the left and then toward the right. The emergency sirens sounded, and Groundhog screamed "man the battle station, man the battle stations! Shunter, give me a full visual please. What the hell was that" As the screen in front of them opened up to its full length and they were able to see directly in front of them, everybody on the bridge stood frozen to the spot, butterfly wings still and rigid.

Blocking the spaceships progress was a swarm of beautifully majestic Seahorses. They were named the Scarlet Seahorses of Saturn, and they were, indeed, the guardians of the planet Saturn. They had come to welcome Groundhog, Shunter and their colleagues. As the two separate sides stood gazing at one another, a voice emanated from space.

" Greetings, please identify yourselves. We are the scarlet seahorses, custodians and protectors of the planet Saturn. You have entered Saturnian airspace, and you need to state your identity and your mission."

"Are all frequencies open Bramdean?" said Groundhog.

"Yes sir" replied Bramdean.

"Hello, many thanks for your friendly greeting" continued Groundhog. "We are a friendly crew of butterflies on a mission from Earth to the Nimbelum, a distant segment of space that you are no doubt familiar with. Our aim is to restore good health to our ailing and very sick mother Tindorella, queen of the entire butterfly population."

The seahorses in front of Sunjammer suddenly started swaying from left to right in a rhythmic, almost poetical manner and were changing colour from scarlet, to red to crimson and then back to scarlet. There was silence for about two minutes and then they spoke, "You have a very long way to travel to the Nimbellum and your objective is very admirable. We have agreed amongst ourselves to give you some assistance and to help you on your way" Groundhog and the rest of the crew looked at one another in surprise and anticipation.

Suddenly, from the tails of the twelve scarlet seahorses positioned in front of the spaceship, there appeared what looked like, twelve very fine, delicate strands of translucent web or hemp, thrusting themselves toward Sunjammer. These strands must have been extremely strong because for the next thirty minutes or so, Sunjammer became totally enmeshed in a multicoloured web. Groundhog and company could only look on in helpless amazement and a certain degree of panic as Sunjammer suddenly began lurching forward at a far greater speed than it had ever achieved.

"We are going to tow you to the other side of Saturn and from there, we will project you toward your destination at a far greater speed than you would normally have managed. There is no need to panic, we are friendly and mean you no harm. We are very much impressed by your kind-hearted attempt to rescue your ailing mother. Just relax and enjoy our planet."

The crew of Sunjammer stood in total silence as the ship travelled at speed. Saturn looked awesome from relatively close. Its butterscotch clouds flew on either side of them, accelerated by Saturn's well known supersonic winds. It was as if they were travelling through and down a vacuum tube. Shooting stars, intergalactic speed demons passed them, and the view and experience was breathtaking, their wings were now fully open, and they were hovering effortlessly and completely at ease within the cramped confines of the spaceship. Many hours passed until suddenly, there was a sudden and violent shudder as Sunjammer began to slow down.

Saturn was behind them now and looking around their 360-degree view, our intrepid crew could see nothing but stardust and space as far as the eye could see. Everything was peaceful when Crystal Tip, the Botanist suddenly said, "Would anyone care for some drinks and refreshments in the resting quarters?"

There was general agreement to this suggestion and Hazelwing, Twiglet, Roebuck and Deadwing accompanied Cristal Tip to the food bar. Meanwhile, back on the bridge, Firefly, Groundhog and Shunter, were assessing and checking for any damage to the spaceship which may have been caused by the huge increase in speed.

"Hello mission control, Bramdean calling from Sunjammer, do you read? Over"

"Hello Bramdean, this is mission control, we read you loud and clear. May we check for any structural damage in the wake of our exciting acceleration surge past Saturn? Over."

"Hello Bramdean, yes that was a huge piece of good fortune wasn't it. The scarlet seahorses of Saturn will forever be enshrined into Butterfly folklore as a species who greatly assisted our mission towards Tindorellas salvation."

Thirty minutes passed whilst mission control checked for any structural damage to the spacecraft.

"Hello Bramdean, this is mission control. Analysis of Sunjammer reveals a few displaced sunflowers and about six acorn cups have been lost but apart from that, she is A okay. Over".

'Okay mission control, do these need replacing or are we okay to proceed? Over."

"Bramdean, you are okay to proceed but please check for any variation in outer core temperature and please be wary of any fragmentation occurring in Sunjammers outer casing. Over."

'That's fine mission control.  Thank you.  Over and out".

The four crew members on the bridge breathed a sigh of relief as Groundhog announced, "Steer a course toward Pluto adjusting lasers and sails, Firefly".

"Very good commander," replied Firefly.

When this last request had been completed, our four heroes put Sunjammer onto automatic pilot and went and joined the others in the restroom for light refreshments of dandelion and elderflower juice supplemented with cupcakes of nettles and Budleigh bush.

"How long before we leave our galaxy and enter the Nimbelum Groundhog?" enquired the navigator Thunderbox.

Groundhog had just wolfed down a cupcake but after gulping it down with a large glass of elderflower juice, he replied "I estimate that if all goes smoothly and according to plan, about four to five days, Thunderbox".

Hazelwing and Twiglet had been busy assessing the overall health and fitness of the entire crew and were satisfied that all was okay and in order. They joined the rest of the personnel and ate refreshments.

A few hours passed as Sunjammer hurtled onwards toward Pluto, its occupants totally unaware that outside in the cold, black vastness of space, space clouds and an increasing quantity of meteorites (fragments of asteroids) had been building. None had actually contacted the ship otherwise the crew would have been immediately alerted. Suddenly, Echoes, the sonar operator was alerted to a bright shimmering display of something to his left as he looked out of the window. It was then that he saw the meteorites hurtling past Sunjammer but it wasn't these that had alerted his attention. What he was witnessing was a space phenomenon called diamond dust. Diamond dust are very small ice crystals, and they were shimmering beautifully in the light being reflected from the planet Uranus.

"Hey everybody, come and take a look at this!" exclaimed Echoes. Practically the entire crew flew over to where Echoes was hovering and looked out in wonder and amazement. It certainly was a beautiful sight but the engineer Shunter, was far more concerned about the increasing cloud and the volume of asteroids.

"Thunderfly and Thunderbox, we need to adjust our altitude and speed immediately in order to avoid these meteorites" ordered Shunter. "Man, all stations, man all stations!!" ordered Groundhog.

The severity of the situation was now apparent as the spaceship started to experience some violent turbulence.

"Groundhog, would it be possible to fire our way through this debris, I mean, to hit the larger chunks", (a giant piece of space junk just missed them) suggested Shunter.

"It may be worth a try. Deadwing (machine gun operator) man the battle stations and set up for some target practice" ordered Groundhog.

Deadwing arranged his guns, took aim and fired in quick succession, ta-ta-ta-ta-ta-ta-bang! He moved his big gun to and fro, from left to right and up and down, shooting down the bigger of the meteorites and containers.

Deadwing was at it for at least an hour. It was of course a joint effort because Firefly was trying to steer a steady course, weaving in and out of the debris and trying to miss the bigger chunks and the navigators Thunderfly and Thunderbox were shouting above the din of the guns, urging Firefly to steer as smooth a course as possible.

Suddenly there was a frantic shout from Echoes," I am picking up a highly unusual, large object to the rear of the ship. It is getting bigger by the minute".

Everybody faced anxiously toward Echoes, "What is it?" shouted Groundhog. "Its volume and strength seem in some way to be connected to Deadwings machine gun firing, commander" explained Echoes.

"Can you identify its composition and mass?" asked Groundhog "Wait a second, oh my God!! exclaimed Echoes, it is made up of meteorite and is growing by the second! "

"Deadwing, stop your firing,"ordered Groundhog.

What in fact was happening to  our  intrepid heroes was that as Deadwing had been firing away and breaking up the bigger chunks of meteorite and by the double existence of zero gravity and a strong magnetism, the smaller chunks were hurtling past Sunjammer and were attaching themselves to each other behind the spaceship and were now posing a huge threat to the ship and crew.

As Deadwing had now stopped firing, the ever-threatening chunks of meteorite were beginning to hit and shake Sunjammer as she slowed right down to a mere 800 miles per hour.

"Battle stations, battle stations would all butterfly personnel please report to the bridge, or if that is not possible would they fasten themselves to the nearest emergency arrestor hook" ordered Groundhog. Within an instant of the order being given, there was a loud bang and dull thud of impact. Sunjammer had been hit! She rolled 360 degrees and tilted violently out of control. Butterflies being as butterflies are, that is having a natural, innate ability to twist and turn, enabled them to simply hover with the impact and so the damage to themselves was minimal.

Sunjammer however, had sustained a direct hit from a comet, those ghastly wanderers of space, dirty snowballs of frozen gas and dust.

The impact pushed the spaceship sideways out of her previous orbit, and she hurtled at great speed through space. As a result of the impact with the comet, two positives had occurred. Firstly, the build-up of comet and meteorite which had formed to the rear of Sunjammer had been left behind and posed no further threat. Secondly, because Sunjammer had been pushed into a different trajectory and was now moving at great speed, (2000 miles per hour to be accurate) she had passed well out of the range and direction of the meteorite shower.

The crew were now back at the controls and frantically trying to slow the spaceship down and to bring her under control.

"Mission control, mission control, do you read? Over." exclaimed Bramdean. "Hello Bramdean, we have you on audio and visual loud and clear. Your co-ordinates suggest that you are way off course. We are assessing the damage to Sunjammer, a few moments please".

There was a sudden silence on the bridge that seemed to last an eternity but after a full thirty minutes there was a crackle and then."Breamdean this is mission control. You have sustained surprisingly little damage, and the spaceship is withstanding your current speed which is much too fast. I suggest that you try to slow down whilst altering your due course. Your position suggests to us that you are heading about thirty degrees off course and approaching the Tarantula Nebula, which is a vast expanse of gas. You are also out of range of the Sun's vital power source which would normally be propelling Sunjammer. Our advice is to rotate your ship at about forty degrees to regain maximum energy from the Sun. You are currently in freefall and out of control. The damage to the ship is no more than a few destroyed sunflowers and some shattered acorn cups. Everything else is intact, and functioning. Over".

"Roger, hearing you loud and clear," replied Bramdean. "We will try our best.  Over and out".

"Okay let's do it," commanded Groundhog." Firefly, can we rotate the ship back to forty degrees enabling our remaining sunflowers to face the Sun?"

"Yes sir, shouldn't be a problem but we need to slow right down" replied Firefly. "Thunderfly and Thunderbox, can you navigate a path to get us back on track", barked Groundhog.

"We will do our best" replied the steely navigators.

With that, the team, over the course of the next forty minutes or so, managed to achieve their objective and bring Sunjammer back on course at a cruising speed of one thousand kilometres per hour. That was the situation for a further three hours. Mission control announced to the crew on board Sunjammer that they had entered the Nimbelum and that in a very short space of time, they would witness the sight of Tindorella and would hopefully be able to assist their universal mother and restore her back to a radiant health and vitality.

"Would all crew members please report to the bridge immediately?" ordered Groundhog.

Within ten minutes the entire crew had assembled on the bridge in two rows, one behind the other. Groundhog continued, "I have been informed by mission control that we have entered the Nimbellum and that in a short while we will have reached our destination and that hopefully, we will be able to help our great mother Tindorella. For this very special occasion and as a mark of respect, I want you all to dress in your finest colours. You have one hour to eat heartily and to make yourselves ready. Please report back here at 16.00 hours ready for action, meeting adjourned".

Everybody was excited as they dispersed, some to the restaurant, others to their rooms.

Suddenly, there was alarm and confusion on the bridge as Echoes exclaimed "Commander sir, I am picking up a very strange image. Come and have a look at this sir".

Groundhog flew rapidly over to where Echoes was stationed and peered at the sonar screen. What they were observing and what they were heading rapidly toward was in fact, a spiral galaxy. It was a rather large, beautiful, natural space entity consisting of multi coloured stars and swirling gas clouds that formed a pattern of at least three long spiral arms curving out from its centre,

"What do you make of it, sir?" remarked Echoes.

"It is a spiral galaxy, very rare for this segment of space. Firefly are you able to reduce speed?" said Groundhog.

After a few seconds, Firefly announced in a panic, "Commander Sir, I am trying but we seem to be locked into a massive energy source which is coming from a central disc within this galaxy".

"As I thought", said Groundhog. "I suspect that we are unable to break free from this and my space sense tells me that we are about to be flung around by one of these large arms and eventually sucked towards the centre or the disc in the middle. I have experienced this only twice in my career as a space commander and so long as we are properly prepared, both the ship and the crew, then we must just ride the lightning and sit it out".

"Bramdean, make a  quick  announcement telling all crew to batten down the hatches, to stop what they are doing and to secure themselves for what will not only be a colourful sight to behold but will be a very bumpy ride".

Bramdean obeyed Groundhog's request, and the commander then turned to Firefly.

"Firefly, would you please secure all parts of Sunjammer that will be sensitive to turbulence and increased speed. That includes all acorn cups and bamboo canes. All butterfly wings are to be flattened and tied as securely as possible to the ship. Could you also draw in Sun jammer's sails and secure them tightly to the side of the ship" ordered Groundhog.

"Aye Aye Sir" signalled Firefly.

Within ten to fifteen minutes this request had been carried out and from the outside, Sunjammer resembled a very large spherical goldfish bowl, hopefully capable of survival at what was about to happen. Whilst all this preparation had been taking place Sunjammer had been sucked deeper into the spiral galaxy and was flying in a circular motion, a sling shot manoeuvre around the disc.

"Thunderfly, Thunderbox what is our current speed" barked the commander. "Sir, current speed 1500 kilometres per hour and increasing", shouted the navigators over the increasing noise caused by the turbulence.

Sunjammer continued to be buffeted for a further two hours. During her journey towards the centre of the spiral galaxy and with the spiral's huge arms encircling her and throwing her around like a baseball, the crew looked out in wonder and amazement as brilliant purple, red and multicoloured stars passed by in all directions. As the sheer force motioned by their speed entrapped them and pressed them hard against the ship's interior, streaks of multicoloured lightning caused by the collision of huge butterscotch-coloured clouds cascaded around the spaceship. And then, all of a sudden, just as Sunjammer seemed in danger of disintegrating. The journey continued but the buffeting and turbulence ceased almost totally, and they seemed to be gliding at great speed, toward the very centre, the disc at the centre of this galaxy.

"Can we assess our location and speed please?" requested Groundhog.

"Sir, current speed is a staggering 7000 kms per hour" announced Firefly. "Commander Sir, I have nothing at all on the screen, a total void" shouted Echoes (sonar operator)

"Sir, our location indicates that we are about to enter the very centre of this galaxy and that the spiral's arms have retreated to their original positions. We are at the outer reaches of the Nimbelum, well inside the fifth quadrant", announced Thunderfly and Thunderbox. (Navigators). "Minimal damage to the ship sir, all crew present and correct sir" announced Shunter (Specialist Engineer).

"Sir there is somebody in the treatment room requiring medical attention, but casualties are minimal" said Twiglet (Chief Nurse).

"Very well, thank you for your reports" barked Groundhog.

Groundhog hovered in a semi relaxed position and thought carefully about the situation. He looked on the positive side. The ship was intact with minimal damage, the crew were in good health and had sustained no serious injury. He asked himself some questions, how close were they to Tindorella and would they be able to help her? After about twenty minutes his thoughts were sharply interrupted.

"Sir, sir" exclaimed Echoes, "I have an unusual image on my screen".

"Put the image on the central screen Thunderfly" requested Groundhog.

" Yes sir" obeyed the navigator.

What the crew observed at this very moment was the outer circumference of the disc at the centre of the Spiral Galaxy which they were now passing through.

"Steady as she goes Firefly" whispered Groundhog.

Sunjammer was cruising very smoothly at great speed, almost gliding. The projection was a beautiful sight to behold. Suddenly a kaleidoscope of colours cascaded past them at great speed, bursting at the extreme edges of the viewing screen. Directly in front of them were a mass of smoking stars, totally harmless, but passing them at great speed. They were in face, rocketing through a wormhole. Wormholes are shortcuts through space. It was a fortunate encounter because they are tunnels which connect one region of space to another. There are apertures at both end, one to enter and one to exit.

"Bramdean" said Groundhog.

"Yes sir" replied Bramdean.

"Could you please contact mission control and ask them for our co-ordinates and our estimated arrival time?", said Groundhog.

"Aye Aye Commander" replied Bramdean.

Within ten minutes mission control had responded and confirmed that they were indeed travelling through an average sized wormhole. The good news for our butterfly warriors was that at the end of this Wormhole lay the very centre of the fifth quadrant of the Nimbelum, where hopefully, Tindorella lay.

"Groundhog, Groundhog this is mission control."

"Reading you loud and clear," replied Groundhog.

"We estimate that your arrival time out of the wormhole and into the Nimbellum to be approximately forty minutes," barked mission control.

"Thanks for that, over and out", replied Groundhog.

After Groundhog had announced to the whole crew that forty minutes would elapse before Sunjammer was eventually clear of the wormhole, all the crew could do was admire and look outside in awe and wonder at the mind-boggling spectacle. One whole hour had passed before things suddenly changed. Suddenly, the spaceship vibrated violently from side to side, knocking some of the crew to the floor and into the walls. The ship and its crew were experiencing at first hand a wormhole exit, which means that they were travelling at great speed on a smooth trajectory one minute and then decreasing speed at a rapid rate whilst experiencing violent turbulence the next. This lasted a good twenty minutes until all of a sudden everything became very smooth with Sunjammer's speed a mere fraction of what it had been.

"Thunderfly, Thunderbox give me a full screen visual", ordered Groundhog.

"Aye Aye sir", replied the very relieved Navigators.

As the screen widened to its full screen capacity, everybody on the bridge gasped and fluttered in

total surprise, wonder and awe. Directly in front of them lay the fifth quadrant of the Nimbellum. It

was populated by an array of space phenomena beautiful to the eye. Such fascinations as, to Sunjammers left, a Polar ring. A Polar Ring is a whole Galaxy with an elongated central body encircled by an end-to-end ring of multi coloured stars. To Sunjammer's starboard side lay a red supergiant, that is a star of huge mass which was actually dying but nevertheless was still a breathtaking sight to behold, several glowing shades of reds and blues that reflected themselves against Sunjammer's sails.

Directly ahead of the ship, and the image that captivated the crew more than any other was a spectacular, large star cluster containing several hundred twinkling stars. The best known of these are the Pleiades and the Seven Sisters, but this was a light show like no other. Sunjammer cruised through these

constellations for a full four hours before she came to a vast, black expanse of open space, a total, vast, blackest of blacks.

"Radio contact with mission control has been lost, I cannot make contact!" said Bramdean.

'My sonar readings are picking up absolutely nothing' announced a worried sounding Echoes.

'Navigation co-ordinates are non- existent; we seem to be locked into an unknown source! We have no control over the ship" exclaimed Thunderfly and Thunderbox in harmony.

"The ship is steering itself sir" explained Firefly.

"There is nothing that we can do but to wait and sit it out," said Groundhog.

At least the ship was gliding smoothly with minimum turbulence. It was very bright inside the spaceship; everything being lit up by the mesmerising spectacles of light outside. This continued for a further two hours and the crew went about their everyday duties and routines. Some went to the restaurant for a slice of lettuce and some berries, others went to the flutter gym to have a workout and to strengthen their wings. Suddenly, there appeared an ominous looking cloud straight ahead. It was coloured a very smoky grey but within it bright lights were flickering and moving at speed. Emerging from the cloud in all directions were space children on an array of cosmic bicycles, trikes, tandems and hybrids. Attached to the front of each bicycle was what looked like a giant bell, each one a different colour and each one flashing a pulse of radiant light, on off on off. The space children wore luminous, reflective spacesuits with very large space helmets. The expressions on their faces were ones of complete joy with radiant smiles. They manoeuvred their machines with total control and as they approached Sunjammer the crew could observe them more clearly. Instead of bicycling in all directions, the space children six in total, had now come together in a row of six facing Sunjammers observation screen.

"Open up visual to maximum" ordered Groundhog. "Control room crew, man your stations and stay on alert".

"Do we have a suitable communications frequency with which to contact these space messengers Bramdean?" enquired Groundhog.

"I am trying Sir, but all radio frequencies appear to be jammed. Wait a minute, they are doing the same and trying to communicate Sir".

The large bell like objects on the front of each bicycle were (among other things, as we shall see later) communication beacons and each bell was giving off a kind of coloured morse code signal, each bell seemed connected to another. It appeared that the space children were communicating with each other. After a while however, all the bells except for one had reduced in intensity to a mere flicker and then,

"Sir I have established radio contact with the group" exclaimed Bramdean suddenly.

"Profound greetings to you" said Groundhog," could you please tell us your name and your mission?"

There was silence for about one minute and then the large bell that had continued to pump out colours and pulses began to glow so brightly that the crew on board Sunjammer were forced to shield their visual antenna from the glow. In addition to this sensation came a guttural noise, that can only be described as the sound of a person gurgling with a mouthwash! There followed a voice so soothing and angelic in its tone and composition that our travellers on the flight deck were both seduced and overwhelmed. So soothing, that Groundhog ordered for all the sound frequencies and channels to be opened so that everybody could hear. Nearly every crew member stopped what they were doing upon hearing this angelic voice and stood motionless, totally mesmerised. Suddenly the voice began to speak.

"Greetings to you all. My name is Condor, I am the leader of this group, and I know who you are and what your mission is all about. I know that you have travelled a vast distance through time and space to rescue and to bring back to life your ailing mother, Tindorella. Well, we are guardians of your mother, and we are here, ready to help you."

Everybody on the flight deck and throughout Sunjammer stood fixed to the spot in total amazement.

"Hello Condor, very pleased to meet you and a huge relief to hear of your friendly manner and intentions to assist us in our quest. Have you seen Tindorella lately, how is she?"

There was a solemn silence between both parties for about a minute before Condor spoke. The angelic smile had disappeared from his and his comrades' faces and had been replaced by a heavy, sombre expression.

"Tindorella is very sick. All her life enhancing lights are nearly extinguished, but she knows that you have organised an earth mission to come to help her and as soon as she heard this news, she seemed to perk up a bit. We are here to guide you to her. You are very close now, no more than a hundred space miles in fact. The Dragonflies as you know, are doing a great job looking after her as best they can and are also fighting off violent cloud formations, meteorites, death stars and other entities seeking to take advantage of and attacking Tindorella in her weakened state. We saw Tindorella two days ago and she is so looking forward to seeing you," said Condor.

Groundhog, Hazelwing and Twiglet were close to tears upon receiving this news, but Groundhog replied, "Many thanks Condor for this latest news. What is the next step? How can you assist us and get us to her as soon as possible?"

"Okay," announced Condor, "what I require you to do within the next thirty minutes or so is to fully prepare yourself, your crew and your ship for a supersonic speed space journey lasting about one hour. This journey, with myself and my team acting as your transportation, will jettison you across the vast Nimbelum to where Tindorella lives and where you can finally assist and hopefully cure her."

Upon receiving this request from Condor, Groundhog set about securing Sunjammer (battening down the hatches, in English naval terms) and informing the entire crew to assume supersonic speed journey formation, that is, probiscis firmly secured to upper body and wings fastened tightly to avoid unnecessary movement or flapping. On the flight deck, a glance at the visual screen witnessed a truly amazing spectacle, courtesy of the cycling children. They had organised themselves into a pyramid shape formation with Sunjammer positioned in the middle, that is two children at the front, one on either side and the remaining two at the back. What was not immediately obvious was that if the crew had happened to glance outside, they would have been very surprised to observe that where once the sky had contained sparkling stars, dust clouds and space debris, a large roughly ovoid shaped area encircling Sunjammer and stretching out for about fifty feet from the spacecraft, was totally devoid of anything except a dull blue grey colour, easily distinguishable from the blue black starkness of space.

What the space children had done was to throw a huge blanket like shawl over our intrepid crew. This was an invisibility cloak that made everything within unseen to anything outside. Suddenly, after about forty minutes, the crew stood transfixed and amazed as the children's bicycles began pulsating a various array of different colours, from electric blue to chocolate brown. These colours were blindingly bright and as they shone brighter Sunjammer began to accelerate at an alarming speed. The butterflies were pinned back against their harnesses as they looked all around them in total bewilderment. It was at that moment that they noticed the lack of anything outside. Acceleration increased for fifteen minutes until it stabilised having reached a colossal speed which was then maintained for the next forty minutes until the spacecraft slowed right down, also coinciding with the bicycles' reduction in colour intensity and thus reverting to their natural hues. Immediately the invisibility cloak was lifted and the sight that greeted the crew outside almost overwhelmed them. Not only had they reached the distant segment of space, the Nimbelum but face to face, directly in front of them was Tindorella herself about one hundred yards away.

The space children had formed themselves three on either side of Sunjammer and communication was finally restored.

"Oh, for the love of butterflies and all creation!!" exclaimed Groundhog.

The entire crew were totally transfixed, tears in every eye as they tried to take in and contemplate what they saw in front of them. There was total silence for at least five minutes until Condor announced,

"There you see before you your poor mother who I can sense, is so very pleased and delighted to see you. Communication is open for you to converse together." Tindorella was hovering almost motionless but for some very faint, shallow breathing. She was situated within a large star cluster of perhaps a thousand twinkling stars of various colours, blue, white, red, yellow, orange and many more besides. Owing to her virtual inability to move she seemed to be trussed up in a complicated network of space webs. These were harmless enough but had accumulated over a long period of time and it appeared that they were holding her captive while in fact the slightest movement could easily disperse them. A far more serious concern was that over time, pulses of intense radiation surges had weakened Tindorella to the point of exhaustion and had had a dramatic effect on her physical appearance. As has been alluded to, almost all of her life lights had been extinguished, and her wings were frayed and torn.

The Dragonflies had done a fantastic job in patrolling and protecting Tindorella over what had been a vast expanse of time. Even at this incredible moment in time the crew were observing them hard at work chasing (at great speed) and hunting down all manner of potential threats, from flying caterpillars glowing in the dark murkiness of deep space to what can only be described as little devils, vivid red in colour with horns and long tails terminating in deadly looking spears or harpoons.

As channels of communication were now open Groundhog and Shunter began to attempt to speak with Tindorella.

"Great mother, great mother of us all, can you hear us? Over."

The words just uttered by Groundhog and Shunter had boomed at such a loud volume outside the spaceship that the whole canopy, the complete scene in front of them appeared to vibrate and distort but there was complete silence. Groundhog once again addressed Tindorella.

"Mother, we have travelled a great distance to come to your assistance and we are so delighted to see you before us, please give us a sign that you can hear us and how we can help. Over."

Another ten minutes elapsed in total silence but then suddenly, the Dragonflies who had been whizzing around and about Tindorella patrolling and chasing potential enemies stopped abruptly and formed a line, every one of them looking toward Tindorella. Tindorella for the first time in what had seemed an eternity, shifted very slightly towards the left. This sudden movement had disrupted all that she was encased in and had sent the network of space webs and thousands of her dead life lights in all directions through the immediate environments of space. It had also created a wind surge sending all this debris slamming against Sunjammer causing her to shudder and sending her occupants flying for cover and stability. The turbulence lasted no more than five minutes but once the dust had settled (so to speak) the most incredible spectacle greeted the crew as they looked out toward Tindorella. The few hundred remaining life cells that she possessed were glowing a beautiful, kaleidoscopic array of multicolours, and then Tindorella spoke for the first time in eons.

'I am very weak; I am very sick, but I recognise your voices and am humbled, for you have travelled a vast distance over space and time to help me in my moment of need. I have sensed your coming and have tried to assist your mission by honing what energy I have left into directing your craft toward me and now that you have arrived, I am so very pleased to see you."

The entire crew were overcome with emotion. They were very overcome indeed. When butterflies become senselessly tearful and affected, they emit a gentle, very feminine lingering humming sound and hover very close to the floor, their wings moving ever so gently to and fro. This was the scene throughout Sunjammers entire interior. Proceedings were brought to an abrupt halt, and discipline was resumed when Groundhog suddenly announced that silence was to be restored so that communication with Tindorella could continue. Bramdean (the radio operator) ensured that frequencies were once again open, and conversation continued.

"Mother, we are all overcome with emotion and are so happy that you can speak with us. Can you please give us an idea of what happened to you to make you so ill and weak?" said Groundhog.

There was no sign or sound from Tindorella for a good ten minutes but then suddenly, a tremendous explosion of light came from her remaining life cells, and this was followed by her voice, but this time it was amplified and almost deafening to the crew of Sunjammer.

"We were hit, we were hit!! we were sucked into a giant black hole, and we saw all manner of dark and sinister manifestations from the past and into the future" screamed Tindorella. Her life cells were shaking violently, and her voice was trembling but after a while things subsided and she was relatively calm.

The entire crew were astounded, some were weeping, others looked distraught."Dear Mother, who were you with, what did you see and who attacked you?" asked Groundhog.

Almost immediately, Tindorella once again lit the sky ablaze and her voice boomed, "I was invited, very kindly invited, to a celestial ball and celebration by my good friends the Horsehead and Crab nebulas. The three of us were rotating and skipping through the cosmos and attracting the most beautiful Pulsars (rapidly rotating neutron stars). We even saw some Quasars forming (a galaxy in the early stages of its evolution). We were really enjoying ourselves when suddenly, we came up against a thick band of very dark Cumulonimbus storm clouds.

As it approached us, the whole band lit up in a blinding white light out of which appeared six space arcs (Asteroids hollowed out with a propulsion system) Behind them, there appeared a very powerful Trifid Nebula (a Photon rocket — a rocket to the stars) Although we were really shaken and tried to communicate with them, the space arcs launched a series of super powerful electrical bursts of energy, like strokes of sheet lightning which tore through us and separated us. The sky was lit up and there were stars exploding but just as the three of us were recovering and beginning to regroup, the space arcs dispersed revealing the Trifid Nebula. It was terrifying to look at and it unleashed what can only be described as a mass of black basalt columns which pushed us backward at great speed, back through the distant reaches of the empty quarter. Before we could steady ourselves, we were violently sucked into Cygnus X-1, a supermassive black hole. We witnessed whole stars speeding past us, together with debris from failed human space missions and other space junk."

Tindorella, whilst narrating her story had become quite hysterical and tearful and as she paused in her rhetoric, Groundhog interjected "Tindorella, our loving mother, please try to calm yourself. We are here to help you and to guide you to restored health. We have brought with us some magic dust and we are praying that it will aid in your recovery"

At this moment, Groundhog summoned Crystal Tip and Roebuck, the climate and botanical experts to locate the magic dust which if you will recall, were housed in six golden caskets, and to bring them into the launching hatch ready for propulsion, aimed at Tindorella. They both knew exactly where the caskets were located having been drilled many times for this precise moment. They were located at the rear of Sunjammer and had been encased in virtually indestructible spider's web. This allowed for some light movement for a slight agitation of the particles themselves to avoid stagnation. Crystal Tip and Roebuck slowly and methodically began to unravel the spider's web, loosening and unclipping each strand until the caskets worked themselves almost free of their moorings. At this point Roebuck went to the back of the pod room, opened an equipment hatch and pulled out a specialized metal case mounted on six sets of rubber wheels. He wheeled it over to where Crystal Tip and the caskets were and positioned it directly in front of them. Roebuck unlocked the metal case to reveal six cylindrical partitions, each one designed to house a ten-inch-long golden casket stuffed with angel dust particles. This was a very delicate operation as Roebuck and Crystal Tip stood, one at each end of the six caskets. There was now just a single, very thick spider's web attached along the bottom, holding all the caskets in at this point.

"Ready, pull!!!" ordered Crystal Tip and with one sharp tug the web broke and all six caskets glided smoothly into their respective partitions inside the metal case. Roebuck secured the cargo and closed the lid.

The launching hatch was situated just beneath the pod room and the metal case was dragged into a lift and lowered into position. When this had been done, Crystal Tip radioed Groundhog to confirm that the caskets were in position, ready for firing. Groundhog spoke to Tindorella, "Dear mother, we are ready to dispatch the magic dust to you.  Are you prepared?"

A brief pause ensued and then Tindorella spoke.

"Dear, dear family and friends of mine. I am so weak and yet I am prepared and ready for this noble and brave attempt."

Groundhog gave the order "Crystal Tip, Roebuck, are you ready?"

"We are ready" came the reply.

"Then fire, fire, fire, fire, fire, fire" ordered Groundhog.

The entire crew were now on the bridge staring at the screen in front of them as the six caskets appeared and arranged themselves in a neat line to the left and right of the spaceship, approximately halfway between it and

Tindorella. The caskets opened and propelled millions of multicoloured dust particles composed of crushed butterfly wings toward Tindorella. She shook, she vibrated and gave out a loud cry, first of joy and then agony as the particles reached her, surrounding and smothering her. It was a sight to behold. She almost disappeared as the magic dust cloaked her in a brilliant shroud of light. It swirled around for about thirty minutes before settling and slowly dispersing. Tindorella came slowly into view, and she suddenly looked radiant. Gone were the jagged edges, the faded colour and the intermittent brightness of her wings. She looked as good as new, and she let out an enormous cry of gratitude and appreciation. The mission had hopefully been a great success. The entire crew felt an overwhelming sense of achievement and happiness, knowing that their mother had been restored to her former strength and vibrancy. They now had to establish what Tindorella's intentions were. Did she want to remain supreme mistress of the Nimbellum or did she want to return home with Sunjammer and the crew.

A large meeting was called on the bridge involving the principal crew members. The screen in front of them was widened to full extent and Tindorella was visible in all her glory, looking magnificent.

"Are frequency channels sharp and well defined Bramdean?" said Groundhog.

"Sound and vision are at maximum Sir" replied Bramdean.

"Tindorella, now that we have managed to restore you to good health and because you look vibrant and happy, may we ask what you intend to do now? What are your intentions?" said Groundhog.

With a flapping of her enormous wings that unleashed thousands of tiny light particles, Tindorella exclaimed "My saviours, intrepid travellers, I intend to return with you and to be much nearer you than I am here in the outer Nimbellum. I have a secret to show you that could only have been performed once I had regained my full powers."

The crew stared at each other in puzzlement and were unprepared for what was to happen next. Tindorella suddenly froze, there was no movement whatsoever. All remaining dust particles had dispersed and the immediate space around her was frozen in time. The crew were also transfixed to the spot not knowing what was coming next. After a couple of minutes, Tindorella appeared to turn in a circular motion. She then turned a full 360 degrees and then stopped, facing the crew of Sunjammer.  Tindorella then turned a full 360 degrees in the opposite direction again coming to a dead stop directly facing the spaceship. What happened next was unbelievable. Tindorella started spinning faster and faster until she resembled nothing more than a long, slightly bulbous sphere. At that moment in time the long sphere that had become Tindorella split into two pieces, one piece enveloping itself within the other thus forming a tightly compact sphere no bigger than a large balloon.

"I have morphed into this size and shape to enable you to accommodate me onto your spaceship for the return voyage" said Tindorella. "You will be able to lock me down condensed as I am now. Essentially, lockdown for the long journey home." added Tindorella.

The crew were astounded by what they had just witnessed, and Groundhog gave the command to prepare the Bee Pods. Sunjammer housed two small landing craft called Bee Pods which were able to fly from the mother ship and land on other surfaces. They were also more than capable of retrieving solid objects because they had ample storage space. They were able to collect Tindorella in bulbous sphere form, bring her back to the ship and lock her down safe and securely, just as she had said. This to pass within a matter of fifty minutes or so.

"Is everybody at their stations and in position?" said Groundhog.

"Aye aye Commander", answered the entire crew as they prepared to leave the outer Nimbellum with their very precious cargo.

"Then plot a course for home Thunderfly and Thunderbox. Maximum wing speed please Firefly" ordered Groundhog.

Their destination was of course Mount Erebus on Antarctica, the take off point from whence this epic space rescue mission had started. They were about two hours into their return flight home when both Shunter and the navigators noticed an unusual feature directly in front of them. The crew had been in a relaxed mood and so was the atmosphere, but everybody was brought to attention by this very large, spectacular site which lay directly in front of them.

"Can we have some more detail on this please?  And could you assist here please, sonar operator?" said Groundhog." This object looks so large and dense that we will be unable to fly around it sir," answered Echoes. "I believe that this is a rather large wormhole, and I am at present unable to determine its exact size and density"

"Give me a reading as soon as you can,"said Groundhog.

Meanwhile. Tindorella, a deck below and hovering toward the rear of Sunjammer had loosened a little and was being attended to and monitored by the medics Hazelwing and Twiglet. There was no dialogue between them, but the mother was under constant surveillance. The medics were amazed by her overall general health considering what she had been through. She seemed delighted to be on board and in the company of her brethren.

About twenty-five minutes had passed since the personnel had reported their findings to Groundhog. "Sir, as we first assumed this is indeed a very long and dense wormhole and we have plotted its start and finish. It starts here and its length is approximately 50000 cosmo metres,  terminating very close to where we need to arrive, namely Mount Erebus on Antarctica. A splendid piece spot of good fortune if I may say so commander," said Echoes.

The atmosphere on the flight deck was a mixture of disbelief and elation at having been informed that all they had to do was to somehow manoeuvre Sunjammer into the eye at the entrance to this massive wormhole. Once this was achieved, then in theory at least, the sheer force of gravity would propel them at a massive speed through the wormhole eventually ending up at the other end and hopefully very near to their final destination.

"Right, Shunter (Engineer), Firefly (Pilot) can you report to my pod in fifteen minutes please", ordered Groundhog.

Firefly put the spaceship on automatic and met the other two as headquarters requested. "What do you think Firefly? Could you control Sunjammer at speed for what would be a lengthy period of time and Shunter, do you believe that Sunjammer has the capacity to withstand huge pressure and force of gravity such as this?" said Groundhog.

Firefly was the first to reply." Sir, if I am not mistaken, once we actually get inside the wormhole the ship will propel itself. All I will be required to do is to steer her and to be wary of any unseen or potential obstacles." Groundhog listened intently, nodding in appreciation at Firefly's intelligent assessment." Sir," mentioned Shunter, "I believe that Sunjammer has the capacity for such an ordeal, but may I suggest that we employ the streamlining and compacting facility so as to maximise Sunjammers slender shape and strength for such a voyage".

A moments silence and then the commander said, 'Thank you very much for your input on this crucial matter, I shall press ahead with preparations for our journey home. Hazelwing and Twiglet, I want you to request that the entire crew undertake a thorough physical and mental workout to ensure that they are in peak condition for the journey home'.

The entire crew were   then assembled in the spacious and opulent Promiscnasium and were subjected to an exhaustive mental and physical conditioning. Groundhog's further instructions were given to Bramdean the spaceship's shapeshifter. His primary responsibility was to change the shape, dimensions and versatility of Sunjammer in any given situation, in this case to streamline and compact the spaceship to give it a maximum chance of success in confronting the wormhole. Four hours later, Bramdean had fashioned Sunjammer into a super slick, strong and pliable object now capable of lightning speed with the ability to bounce from solid objects such as walls with minimum damage to her infrastructure. With the crew in tip top condition and Sunjammer primed, she was ready to be positioned directly over the wormhole.

"All essential personnel please take your positions in the control room", ordered Groundhog.

A bustle of activity commenced as they took up their positions and strapped themselves in, their wings securely clamped against their bodies.

"Are we ready? Okay Firefly, please centre us directly over the wormhole entrance, proceed with caution, we don't want to sustain any avoidable damage to our ship," said Groundhog.

Sunjammer glided gently at first, slowly rotating herself as she moved towards the entrance but then turbulence! She was confronted by very strong resistance pushing her back in the direction from where she had come but with plenty of perseverance and piloting skills, Firefly managed to get the spacecraft

into position. Firefly was now holding Sunjammer in a hovering position, the engines were idling at minimum warp speed (treading water if you like) or in butterfly terminology, stationary flapping or motionless manoeuvring. For Sunjammer to be sucked into and taken up by the vortex or power stream of the wormhole, all engines had to be turned off.

"Firefly cut all engines" ordered Groundhog

An eerie silence descended on the flight deck as the engines were shut down. The view in front of them was awesome. Deathly silence, deathly stillness over the mouth of this huge wormhole. You could not hear a wing flap. This position was maintained for a full ten minutes but then gradually, a noise, followed by a vibration, grew louder and fiercer as Groundhog was heard shouting "Brace brace brace"

Sunjammer lurched forward at quite an acute angle and was at that moment of impact sent into the vortex and down the wormhole at superfast speed.

Once inside the wormhole however, they seemed to be floating as the sensation of speed virtually stopped even though they were moving at great speed. Outside, all around them was a wonder of colour and light, The walls of the wormhole were composed of Basalt, Cubelets of Sulphur, the rock crystal Quartz, very colourful Jasper stones and beautifully layered sections of Agate. Ahead of them and showering them as they moved through them, were masses of tiny sky blue Celestite crystals. They were lit up by the Sulphur decorating the wormhole walls.

The entire crew stood mesmerized and transfixed at the awesome sight. After some considerable time, the shower of Celestite crystals subsided to reveal a rather more menacing sight. Sunjammer was surrounded by what appeared to be a large mass of black ball bearings. These were covered in thick stems with broad suction mats at  the  end of each stem. They were rotating very slowly but appeared stationary even though they and Sunjammer were moving at great speed.

"Bramdean, please open all communication frequencies" ordered Groundhog. As the frequencies were opened Groundhog announced "Hello, this is Groundhog, spaceship commander. We have successfully carried out an important rescue mission and are heading home to Earth. Please identify yourselves, who are you and where are you from?"

It wasn't long before the crew on the flight deck could hear a faint, pulsating beat similar to a human heartbeat. Over the course of a few minutes, it grew louder and then stopped. Then someone spoke.

"We are the Coronisidis and we are from a region on Mars called the Isidis Plantitia. You have entered a non-neutral wormhole zone. This territory belongs to the Thaumasians of the western hemisphere of Mars and as protectors of this region, we are assigned the task of repelling and if necessary, of attacking all trespassers. Please turn back immediately!"

There was complete silence on the flight deck as the crew looked at one another and then toward the large outside screen that by now, was filled and swarming with sinister looking Coronisidis. These creatures had the ability to communicate with each other using telekinesis and decisions therefore were made that could not be picked up by the crew of Sunjammer. Butterflies, however, have a similar way of communicating, invisible to others, by a multiple flapping of their wings and also by intricate dance movements such as hovering and moving from side to side. There was a stalemate. Nothing was said for a full ten minutes until the Coronisidis made a sudden move. They all grouped together, spread out and formed a circle, surrounding Sunjammer whilst at the same time gaining height, creating some distance between themselves and the spaceship. Things were still  for a moment, but then multiple thud thuds were felt and heard on Sunjammers outer casings as the Coronisidis began dive bombing and attaching themselves to the ship. The Coronisidis could be seen flying high and dive bombing again, attaching themselves in even greater numbers.

"Activate the second skin, activate the second skin Shunter" barked Groundhog.

The second skin was an ultra- strong internal layer of battle-hardened fabric composed of Stone, Iron and Pallasite Meteorite which could withstand just about anything, and it had been incorporated into the ship's construction. As Shunter carried out the order, a dark shiny substance began to form around the whole inner surface area of the spaceship. After about half an hour the inner surface was completely covered, as complete a form of defence as the ship could muster.

The crew continued their journey home, but by now, swarms of Coronisidis had detached themselves from the ship. The large screen in front was now completely clear of Coronisidis and Groundhog assumed that the second skin fixed to the interior had done the job and had secured and protected the inhabitants within. The threat had been defeated. Nothing could have been further from the nut. The crew stationed throughout the ship had all noticed the tiny indentations that had appeared through the second skin. The composition of the Coronisidis was such that protruding from their ball bearing like bodies were slippery tentacles reaching in all directions. At the end of each of these tentacles were suction pads and emerging from these pads were razor sharp points capable of penetrating the strongest and most resistant of defences. Sunjammer was an easy prey. It was not long before the indentations had penetrated right through and appeared as tiny square portholes, protruding into the ship. This caused great alarm among the ship's company and the control room was in a state of near panic.

Within minutes Groundhog had ordered Shunter and some of the technicians to one area of the ship which had a particularly dense cluster of portholes, so as to assess the damage. Using long spatulas and even longer probes they attempted to take a small sample from one of the sinister looking apertures. As they were attempting this, they noticed a very unpleasant smell. The smell was actually fraying their wings and was even sending one or two of them into violent convulsions. The Coronisidis were discharging an invisible gas capable of paralysing and disarming insects but especially butterflies and it was being released through the portholes.

Shunter called to Groundhog "Sir, the Coronisidis are emitting a highly toxic gas that is making us all very drowsy, sick and is affecting our physical appearance ".

"Hazelwing,, Twiglet, proceed to deck C Room 15 (which was the chemical warfare concentration room, CWCR) and in the drawer marked Anti Attack Red Annihilator Matter (AARAM) take out the seven red vials which are housed in a white ceramic Belleek container and await my further instructions," said Groundhog.

"Very well sir" answered the chief medics.

Shunter and his team had put on anti-gas chrysalis and were totally covered and protected by this impressive piece of kit. The gas was at this point being discharged throughout the ship and its crew were becoming ill and weak, its effects were fraying their wings and turning fern an array of different colours. It took Hazelwing and Twiglet about fifteen minutes to reach the CWCR, open the drawer named AARAM and take out the container housing the seven red vials.

"We have the vials in front of us" announced the medics to Groundhog.

"Excellent, now I want you to proceed directly to the diffusion room and await my further instructions".

Hazelwing and Twiglet had never been in the diffusion room before, so when they arrived and opened the door, they were just a little taken aback. It was a medium sized room, completely empty and bare except for an impressive looking glass structure, not unlike a chandelier, which hung suspended from the ceiling. Suspended from this were seven very long crystal chains, separated from each other by two, thick golden wheels, positioned roughly three feet apart from each other. Attached to each chain and hovering about a foot from the floor were seven silver petri dishes each containing a different coloured substance, the composition of this substance as yet unknown.

"Have you reached the diffusion room yet?" asked Groundhog.

"Affirmative Commander, we are inside now" answered Hazelwing.

"Okay, hover over to the glass structure at the centre of the room and very carefully place the Belleek container directly in front of the seven petri dishes. When this is done, I want you to very carefully remove each vial in turn, hover over to each petri dish in turn and pour (diffuse) the contents of the   vials into the petri dishes. Don't be alarmed by the reaction, this will produce a fizzing sound, and smoke will rise from the dishes. Once this is done, flutter back about four feet and wait for the reaction. Don't panic and don't be alarmed at what appears. These are our friends and allies, and they will give us an above average chance of success against the Coronasidis" said Groundhog.

Hazelwing and Twiglet looked at each other in complete bewilderment. Little did they know that this had never been attempted before and that this was Sunjammers secret weapon against any hostile aggression committed by alien forces. They did as they were instructed and stood at each end slowly diffusing the contents of each vial into the dishes. They met in the middle, hovered back and awaited the outcome. They didn't have to wait long for within ten minutes, a loud, crackling and fussing sound began emanating from the dishes. This sound was accompanied by thin plumes of smoke, each plume a different colour hovering above the dishes. These were unusual in that the smoke only rose a couple of feet or so and then lay in virtual suspension, swirling slowly. It was a beautiful sight to behold but emerging from the plumes of smoke there suddenly appeared seven pairs of light mottled brown coloured wings. Moments later seven fearsome looking bodies about three inches long with spindly but robust hairy legs, appeared out of the smoke. A loud buzzing noise was heard as Hazelwing and Twiglet stared in disbelief. All seven insects turned and faced them head on.

"Commander, commander" shouted Hazelwing.

"Do not panic and don't be afraid," said Groundhog. "Allow me to introduce you to our very powerful and formidable allies, the Vespa Hornets".

(Vespa Hornets are part robotic and part insect. They were originally discovered in great numbers on the planet Vespasian and are very formidable fighting machines. When it was discovered that they could be transported in liquid form and could therefore occupy a minimum of space, they were included in Sunjammers armoury. They were to be called upon only in an extreme emergency, but that time had unfortunately arrived. The Vespa Hornets communicate with one another by using a variety of pitches heard only by themselves. Their weaponry includes potent sangers about an inch long, capable of paralyzing their victim long enough for the Hornet to get close enough to totally destroy it. Its central weapon, however, is its unique ability to give off an acidic scent which dissolves everything in its path. The Vespa Hornet has an indestructible outer shell.

Groundhog was able to communicate with the Vespa Hornets using a complex range of buzzing frequencies.

"Shunter, would you please activate the aperture tunnel and release the Vespa Hornets" ordered Groundhog.

"Tunnel activated" replied Shunter.

The aperture tunnel was located in the centre of the ceiling directly above the glass structure in the diffusion room and it connected that room to the outermost post of Sunjammer and beyond that , to the vastness of space.

There were apertures at each end and Shunter had just opened them. Groundhog suddenly tilted himself to one side and hovered over to a tiny cubicle located in one corner of the flight deck. Once inside, the crew could observe him gliding very gently from side to side and could also hear a quick succession of pitched buzzes, from very high to very low.

Back in the diffusion room, Hazelwing and Twiglet stood transfixed as the Vespa Hornets turned around and one after the other, flew upwards and out of the opened aperture, along the tunnel and out through the second aperture and into space. They were clear of the spaceship and were now confronting the Coronasidis. The Coronasidis were making an unearthly noise, a squawking sound not unlike thousands of magpies alerting one another over the presence of food. Having observed the Vespa Hornets facing them, the squawking stopped only to be replaced by a deafening silence. There must have been thousands of Coronasidis, most of them hovering around Sunjammer but a sizeable minority had attached themselves to the ship and were eating and boring their way through the ships outer shell. The Coronasidis attacked first by elevating themselves in unison and swirling around Sunjammer, not unlike the Starlings 'murmur'. They then organised themselves into the shape of a vast arrow and one could see that their ball bearing shaped outer bodies had changed into sleek, harpoon shaped fighting machines. Their tentacles had retracted into their bodies and their arrow shape contained within it, bright, red mini furnaces of fire and fury. Within a few seconds the mass had picked up momentum and was hurtling toward the Vespa Hornets. The Hornets had arranged themselves into a line from front to back resembling a snake with a slight curve in the centre. The Coronasidis were no more than one hundred yards from the Vespa Hornets and were closing in fast. They had to do something immediately and they didn't disappoint. Seven stingers were deployed and were fired at the Coronasidis. Attached to these stingers were extremely tough flexible nets that unfurled when in close contact with an enemy. They then attached themselves into one large net that surrounded the large, offensive arrow of the incoming Coronisidis and stopped it in its tracks. As the net tightened, the Coronisidis seemed to be in total disarray, the precise arrow shape of their mass disintegrated into fragmented broken clusters. This was followed by the frightening sound of squawking and screaming. At the same time, the Vespa Hornets had flown to within fifty feet of the enemy and were ready to unleash their primary weapon. The Coronasidis were strapped in an inescapable net, they had been broken up, their small red mini furnaces of fire and fury had been all but extinguished and they were now at the mercy of the Hornets. The Hornets could be heard communicating (buzzing) to one another and this scenario lasted for about one hour by which time all seven Hornets had elevated their metallic wings at exactly the same time to about one foot above their torsos. Their wings were composed of several overlapping layers of reinforced titanium. Each layer had two apertures, one at each end. All at once, the apertures opened together and began releasing a visible, very acidic powder with a very strong scent. This was fired at the Coronisidis and was intended to surround them and to penetrate them from the outside. Whilst the powder was being deployed the Vespa Hornets unleashed a terrifying arsenal of stingers, grenades and fireballs aimed directly at the central mass of the enemy. It didn't take long for the acidic powder to do its job because clearly visible to both the Vespa Hornets and the crew of Sunjammer was the sight of the disintegration of the Coronisidis. Its central mass was imploding, reducing it to a black tarlike substance which was beginning to drip and fall away. The stingers, grenades and fireballs were successfully destroying the frontlines and this sustained attack ensured that Sunjammer could continue on its journey home.

Everybody on board Sunjammer had been watching the action from the moment the Vespa Hornets had launched their attack until the  final destruction of the Coronasidis. Cheers and jubilation had turned into shock and disbelief at the sight in front of them. Whilst the Hornets had done a fantastic job in destroying the frontlines and using the acidic powder to dissolve and break up the main body of the Coronisidis, it quickly became apparent that the bulk of the enemy had been surrounding and protecting a sinister entity within. Very similar to worker Bees surrounding a hive to protect the Queen. The entity was called Ascuris and it was now exposed. It was the mother chieftain and master of the Coronisidis. It had a black organic, circular body roughly fifty feet in diameter and it was covered in bright red thick tentacles radiating, some twenty feet out into space. At the end of these tentacles were very furry apertures or gaping holes. The tentacles were not rigid but flexible and were waving as though in freefall. This creature dwarfed Sunjammer. Its body was covered in wings or flaps, and it possessed three long, red tails each terminating in an object resembling a ships anchor. The Ascuris was moving very slowly on its own axis. It possessed two very large eyes. and the iris and pupils were a very bright sunset yellow.

The Vespa Hornets were immediately alerted to this new threat and moved themselves into position at lightning speed, no more than thirty feet away and facing them head on. They were tiny compared to the Ascuris but their sudden positioning prompted the Ascuris to turn and face them head on. The Vespa Hornets had been communicating between themselves for some time when suddenly, they unleashed all their weaponry including the acid powder which was pouring from the apertures in their wings. On this occasion however, it had no effect whatsoever. The Ascuris had deployed a protective shield that completely surrounded it and rendered the Hornets weaponry useless. The acid powder was broken down upon impact and when the Hornets fired the stingers and grenades at the Ascuris, they just exploded upon impact with the shield. None of them got through. Whilst this was going on, the Ascuris had rotated so that its three long tails were facing the Vespa Hornets. Suddenly the tails began swishing quite forcefully from side to side and in a split second, the anchors at the end of each tail had reared up and attached themselves to three of the Hornets. With a huge circular motion the tails of Ascuris catapulted the Hornets far out into space where they crashed and exploded into some distant sulphur structures. The four remaining Hornets turned around in the direction of Sunjammer and were attempting to escape this desperate situation by moving at full throttle when they became ensnared in the Ascuris's three tails and were held fast by these powerful magnets. One swish of its tails sent the four remaining Hornets hurtling into the void and smashing into some electric blue rock formations. The crew of Sunjammer now stood fearing for their lives. As for the Coronisidis, every last one of them had been completely destroyed and because of that the Vespa Hornets would be hailed as martyrs. The looming presence of the Ascuris now faced them head on. Radio frequencies were opened and for a full hour, Bramdean, Shunter and Groundhog attempted to make audible contact with the Ascuris but without success. The alien had been rotating slowly during this period and had turned 360 degrees but with excellent ocular capabilities it always had Sunjammer in its sights. The Ascuris was completely mute and could only communicate with the Coronisidis via a series of subtle movements, with its eyes and with its many tentacles.

Suddenly, the Ascuris lurched forward taking the crew by complete surprise. It wasn't moving at speed but what was concerning was that four of its flailing tentacles were attempting to surround Sunjammer. It moved closer and closer until a large jolt was felt throughout the spaceship. Ascuris had Sunjammer in its steely grip as four of its tentacles had wrapped themselves around it and the viewing screen on the flight deck was filled by an enormous pair of sunset-coloured eyes staring at the crew.

"Firefly, move engines to full throttle" ordered Groundhog.

"She won't budge an inch sir" replied Firefly.

"Then reverse engines at full speed," said Groundhog.

"She won't budge sir" replied Firefly.

"Then it would appear that we are being held against our will by this demon from Mars" announced a rather dejected Groundhog.

"Bramdean, can you attempt once more to establish contact with it," said Groundhog.

Bramdean opened all frequencies and made numerous attempts to communicate with the Ascuris but to no avail. It had the spaceship in a vice like grip. Three hours passed without any contact, and this had allowed Groundhog and his senior staff time to retire to the conference room and figure out their next move. Whilst all of this had been taking place, the rest of the ships' company who were scattered throughout Sunjammer had been observing events from every porthole and every available viewpoint. All these viewpoints had now been covered by the Ascuris's bulking mass. Some of the butterflies obtained close views of its body, others of its menacing looking tentacles and others still of its long, red tails. There was however, one location where there was still a clear view outside. At this precise location, its body was to the north and a giant tentacle was to the south and the angle in between provided a clear view into space. The two crew members who had been observing events from this porthole were Grayling and Ringlet, both engineering technicians. This porthole happened to be located directly above the pod distribution and storage bay, the very location where Tindorella was resting after her arduous experience. Grayling and Ringlet were again casually looking out of this porthole when they were suddenly startled by an unexpected event. At first, they saw two very powerful beams of light coming from directly below them. A few moments later they were amazed to see a bee pod in full view of them and moving out and away from Sunjammer. Grayling was in communication with Groundhog on the flight deck. "Commander, commander, you won't believe what Ringlet and I have just seen. One of the bee pods has just left the ship!"

Groundhog was astounded as he ordered two of the crew to fly to the pod room to verify what Grayling had just said but also to see that Tinderella was comfortably secured in her hammock. It didn't take long before the information was confirmed and that one of the bee pods had indeed been jettisoned away from the ship. Something else was missing, however.

Tindorella had managed to wriggle free from her moorings and was piloting the escaped bee pod. When this was reported back to Groundhog, he was both shocked and saddened as were all the crew. What was Tinderella doing?

Did she realise the danger she was in? The Ascuris dwarfed Tinderella and the bee pod and a swish of one of its tails or a steely grip from a tentacle could destroy Tindorella and she would perish just like the Vespa Hornets. The incredible journey and rescue of Tindorella would all have been in vain. The crew on the flight deck had barely taken in what had happened when something truly amazing happened right before their eyes. As you will recall, the Ascuris had embraced Sunjammer with a grip of steel, its tentacles wrapped firmly around the spaceship and its large penetrating eyes literally pressed against the large ships monitor directly in front of the personnel on the flight deck. These eyes had since blinked two or three times and had glanced to the left and to the right. There was a sudden jolt, the pair of eyes moved away and the Ascuris had loosened its grip on Sunjammer. Tindorella had distracted it by flying around the Ascuris who had turned 180 degrees and was directly facing the bee pod and Tindorella. Sunjammer was positioned to the right of Tindorella at the same altitude, with the Ascuris a long way to the left also at the same altitude (imagine Sunjammers position on a corner flag at a football ground with Tindorella in the near half and the  Ascuris positioned in the furthest half). Directly behind Sunjammer and for as far as the eye could see, there lay mountains and canyons of Sulphur, Quartz and Ice crystals. Everything was still and silent within this giant wormhole when suddenly the bee pod started vibrating to such an extent that parts of it began to fall away and disintegrate. After fifteen minutes it was gone but then a most beautiful sight, Tindorella emerged, wings fully extended and this time she was huge, two to three times her original size.

Her colours shone a  hue of purples, pinks, greens and blues but her dominant colours were now black and scarlet and it was these colours that were pulsating, looking very menacing and aggressive. Dark shades of black lined her wings and scarlets and reds radiated throughout her body. Tindorella was emitting a series of high pitched, blood curdling screams directed at the Ascuris. The Martian was motionless except for his tails and tentacles which were swaying in a rhythmic, almost poetic motion as if it were conducting a cosmic orchestra, however one look into its large eyes betrayed its calmness and revealed its true intentions. The sunset-coloured eyes which had entranced the crew had now turned the colour of Basalt and Copper. Fury and anger were revealed in them as the Ascuris prepared to attack Tindorella and to beat and poison her into submission and eventual destruction. Tindorella struck first. From a series of pocket like pouches which lay inside her body, she released long umbilical like coils that flicked out towards the Ascuris and made contact with its torso, delivering a series of high voltage electric shocks. The Martian was taken by surprise and visibly recoiled, letting out a terrifying aaaarrreeee, before stabilizing itself and once again facing Tindorella. The Ascuris suddenly unleashed two of its flailing tentacles toward Tindorella, striking both of her wings with such force that fragments of wing, vein and fibre broke away from her body and dissolved into the void of space. This attack had lurched Tindorella's body to the left, rendering her wingspan severely compromised and leaving her vulnerable to another attack. A second attack came almost immediately as the Ascuris directed both of its tails toward Tindorella, its two anchor finials attaching themselves to her body. It then attempted to pull her towards it using all of its strength to try to subdue and then consume her.

Tindorella however, was putting up a fierce resistance and they were playing tug of war for over thirty minutes. The Ascuris was getting the better of Tindorella and she was now crying out in desperation and was trying to maintain an even keel considering the sheer strength of the enemy. The Ascuris thought that it had won the battle and was looking forward to a Tindorella toastie. It was bitterly disappointed because Tindorella had other ideas. As she was being slowly drawn toward the Ascuris and was continuing to try to struggle free, her whole body including her damaged wings suddenly began to vibrate with such ferocity that the Ascuris was now struggling to keep a firm grip on its prey. In a second, the hues of purples, pinks, greens and blues of Tindorella had contained an arsenal of different shaped, very small flint arrowheads. The arrowheads were coloured the same as her colours, so they were concealed within her and were now deployed to maximum effect. Tindorella fired all of them towards the sulphur mountains and canyons that lined the wormhole on both sides. The peculiar designs of the arrowheads meant that when fired at a particular angle and upon impact with the sulphur, not only would it ignite but it would break off and return at great velocity and accuracy towards its intended target, in this instance the Ascuris. This is exactly what happened.

(A small footnote about the production of the flint arrowheads. They are not composed of 100% flint but are as hard as flint. It was possible to produce them because the angel dust that the crew of Sunjammer had brought with them to save Tindorella had in it a substance which when combined with very fine white quartz crystals, a type found only in the Outer Nimbellum, could form a substance that could be moulded into lethal 'flint' arrowheads. These will instantly ignite when in contact with sulphur)

Hundreds of ignited sulphur splinters crashed headlong into the Ascuris and began burning into its vast body. It immediately loosened its grip on Tindorella, its tentacles and its two tails retracted back into its body, and it let out a painful cry that shook Tindorella and Sunjammer. The splinters continued to pump into the alien for a good ten minutes until it finally relented and retreated at great speed back down the giant wormhole. The crew of Sunjammer had been observing the whole spectacle with a mixture of fear, excitement and anticipation and were very much relieved when they saw the Ascuris fading out of sight. Their pressing urge now was to come to the aid of Tindorella. She had been badly wounded with lacerations on her wings. They were about to try to communicate, and Groundhog was about to issue the order to release the remaining bee pod to assist Tindorella when something remarkable happened. The dust had just begun to settle outside after the battle, the space dust that had been whipped up was beginning to distil into the night when suddenly, Tindorella opened up her wings to their maximum capacity and expanded her body fully. It was as though she was enjoying a well- earned stretch. It also exposed the damage that she had sustained at the hands of the alien. The tips of her black and scarlet wings had been shredded and there were some gaping, serious looking wounds to her torso. She appeared to be in some pain when she turned 45 degrees so that she was facing the range of sulphur crevasses to which she had so successfully fired the flint arrowheads. She hovered, staring at them for a while and then in a flash, the complete outline of her body began to glow a wonderful electric blue. Her damaged sections were glowing a lot brighter, and she started swaying from side to side. It looked as if she was communicating with the Sulphur canyon. After a while, the canyon began secreting some small white crystals that floated, gently and soothingly around the space between it and Tindorella. They dust were moving toward her, and she seemed to be inviting them to her. These small white crystals had the power to heal Tindorella completely and when they eventually reached her and made contact, the result was breathtaking. The quartz crystals attached themselves to her damaged parts and a fusion of crystal and butterfly dust created a dense fog within which an array of colours spat out and swirled around.

Nothing much could be seen of Tindorella for a while but then the fog cleared. Tindorella appeared, completely healed, her damaged parts as good as new. She spread her wings and flapped them six or seven times to dispel the loose, dead skin but also to circulate air around the freshly healed wounds. She then turned to face Sunjammer, her movement and flexes suggesting that she wished to communicate with the crew. Groundhog sensed this and motioned to Bramdean,

"Bramdean, open all communication frequencies please."

"Tindorella, can you hear me?" asked Groundhog.

"I can hear you and I wish to offer my assistance. Please listen to me because we don't have much time. This wormhole is highly unstable and is in imminent danger of collapse. Listen to my instructions and act immediately" motioned Tindorella.

The crew on the flight deck were very alarmed at what had just been said but remained steadfast and awaited Groundhog's instructions.

"Attention all personnel, attention all personnel" announced Groundhog.

"Wherever you are, located around the ship, please remain still and don't move and await my further instructions".

Tindorella spoke again. "Groundhog, could you please instruct Firefly, your pilot, to steer Sunjammer to a position directly behind me and then to await further instructions."

Groundhog acted immediately and ordered Firefly to steer the ship behind Tindorella. This took no time at all. All was quiet for a while except for the distant rumble of the volcanic mountains which were disintegrating at an alarming rate. A few, giant lumps of quartz and ice that looked dangerously close had also begun to fragment and were spewing tiny fragments out towards Sunjammer hitting it from time to time but causing minimal damage.

"Groundhog, Shunter and every crew member onboard, you saved me from a certain death, you restored me to optimum health and vitality, and you have brought me thus far towards our journey's end, where we shall once again find the lush, green woodland, fields, forests and meadows of our mother, Earth. I wish to repay you now because as you will observe, we are in a grave situation, but we are not so far from home" said Tindorella.

Groundhog issued an announcement "Would all personnel please find the nearest nectar station (there were plenty of these throughout the ship, they were small bubble/pod rooms where an individual butterfly could house himself very securely. There was enough food in them to last five days and each pod was attached to a wall within the spaceship) and secure themselves firmly. Be prepared for this to be your home for forty-eight hours at least"

There was a boisterous flurry of activity throughout the ship as many scores of butterflies flew around, locating the nearest nectar station and settling themselves inside.

The view from the bridge was startling. Tindorella was positioned about one hundred metres from Sunjammer and she looked beautiful having been restored to good health. Her wings were fully extended and her body looked firm and powerful, a shocking hue of crimson and electric blue which stood out against the black backdrop of space.

Suddenly, appearing from the stark outline of her black and scarlet wings, hundreds of strands of wafer thin, millifiore (glass) superstrong threadules began to cast out towards Sunjammer, surrounding and attaching themselves to her. She was slowly but surely being pulled toward Tindorella. After about twenty minutes, the spaceship was totally encased in fine glass threadules and was pressed firmly but safely into Tindorella's strong body. For added protection, Tindorella had produced small but strong, feathery fins that overlapped each other, and which were positioned across Sunjammer. They were now ready to escape the disintegrating wormhole and to head for home. With one huge effort, Tindorella let out a piercing cry, flapped her wings and moved forward at great speed away from imminent danger and down through the wormhole. She had to fly very carefully indeed, dodging falling rutile quartz crystals shaped like arrowheads that were detaching themselves from the sides of the wormhole. These were likely to penetrate her wings if she caught one accidentally. Another potential danger that was releasing itself from the wormholes walls was the crystal called Natrolite. It forms into long columns and is attracted to heat. The heat produced by the flapping of Tindorella's wings was an obvious target and if it attached itself, it would fuse and grow, and its weight would severely hamper the flight home. Tindorella was aware of these perils and evasive action was needed on several occasions.

The personnel on board Sunjammer were engaged in various pursuits whilst Sunjammer was navigating a way home. Rosehip and Cedarwood were playing a game of flight wing fortunes and Grayling and Ringlet (our engineering technicians) were amusing themselves by studying blueprints of Sunjammers technical capabilities.

After two days and two nights of dodging projectiles and weaving and diving at great speed, Tindorella began to slow down and eventually came to rest on a large ledge made of Gypsum (a mass of columnar crystals). Directly in front of her was a vast opening, the end of the wormhole had at last been

reached. Through the opening, far as the eye could see, a vast expanse of lush, green forest with a wide, meandering river dividing it could be seen. Tindorella informed Groundhog of their safe landing and relative safety and Groundhog duly announced to the ship's crew that they were safe to unharness themselves and to vacate the nectar stations. There were scenes of frenetic activity as the butterflies fluttered up to the windows to get a view of what lay outside. Tindorella immediately released Sunjammer by releasing the feathery fins which had been positioned over the glass threadules. She then began to generate an intense heat which had the effect of melting the glass threadules and thus releasing Sunjammer from Tindorella's firm grip. The spaceship flew immediately towards the lush, green forest that butterflies are naturally attracted to and landed on a large area of green grass.

Everything was very sunny, there was no wind at all and as they surveyed their surroundings there lay a scene of beauty and different shades of green. They had no idea of where they were in the cosmos but there was an uneasy feeling amongst them that things were not as they seemed and that something was not right.

The trees looked lush and there were all sorts of varieties and species, but they were too orderly. They didn't seem real and resembled a standing army. There were four huge yew trees, and they were positioned one at each corner of the large, almost square expanse of green grass. Another thing that they noticed was that beyond the line of trees (beautiful as they were) and looking at eye level through them, there was no horizon, the land seemed to completely disappear. After a lengthy pause, Groundhog gave the order,

"I want you all to fan out and fly as far as you can flutter and then report back to me. I need to know what lies beyond these trees which surround us on all sides."

There was a bit of a commotion as most of the ship's crew, a multi-coloured spectacle, swooped and glided through the trees. Groundhog, Shunter, Firefly and Ringlet were the only ones left. After about one hour, a woosh could be heard among the Cedars, Poplars, Beech, Sycamore and Ash trees as the butterflies returned en masse with some startling news.

'Sir, we flew as far as we could only to discover that beyond the line of trees over there to the north is an edge and then complete blackness. The sky seems to turn from a deep sky blue to a cold darkness' said Deadwing. 'Yes sir, we found the same thing to the south' echoed Twiglet. The group that had flown to the eastern and western edges repeated the same thing.

Groundhog and the others now knew that something was amiss.

Tindorella had been silent and still for a while but suddenly, she swooped down and was hovering above them.

"Hello everybody, you are correct, nothing is as it seems' announced the great mother. 'I have been flying around this location and have discovered that the area of greenery that we have landed on is in fact a highly unstable block of meteorite but a very pliable and fertile block, which during its very lengthy existence has come into contact with green earth pods, causing its surface to grow the most beautiful flora and fauna. The good news is that we are nearly home, and the bad news is that we must get off this deceptive rock as soon as possible."

Groundhog and the entire crew stood silent and very still. It was as if they had suddenly been turned to tortoise shell stone.

Just at that moment, the fertile meteorite began to shake and all the trees surrounding it began to shake quite violently. This friction didn't uproot them as one would expect instead, they began to quietly lean over and lay flat on the ground. As they looked around them, they could see that the whole landscape had flattened except for the four yew trees. Amazingly, these had lit up into bright silvery orbs and were pulsating on and off, just like a lighthouse projecting its beam far out to sea. The outer edges to which the butterflies had flown had raised some form of protective shield which meant that they were now encased in a very large rectangular box. This was a transportation container. Groundhog gave the order, 'Would all personnel secure themselves to the nearest nectar pod and prepare for some turbulence'.

Whilst the order was being carried out, a rather large cover, constructed from a mass of long, spindly tree roots and branches had completely covered the rectangular box in which they were trapped. The box was now in motion and moving at quite a pace. Once again, they could only stare in wonder as they passed star clusters and formations shrouded in a space of utter blackness. The yew trees were flashing on and off and to the great relief of everybody on board, Tindorella could be seen flying and swooping alongside, looking as if she was thoroughly enjoying herself.

Groundhog requested the co-ordinates and position of Sunjammer, to get some idea of where they actually were and was amazed at the reply.

Bramdean, the radio operator, Thunderfly and Thunderbox, the navigators and Echoes, the sonar operator all confirmed that they were now within the Solar System and were positioned between the Earth and the Moon. The strange earthen, rectangular box complete with yew trees for beacons was taking them home. The good news was relayed throughout the ship and the reception was one of huge relief and jubilation. They were somewhat at the mercy of the strange box in which they were encased but everyone had a strange butterfly feeling that they would be okay and that the box would deliver them safely. Having Tindorella flying alongside was a great comfort for them, but questions needed to be answered.

How would the box cope with the intense heat generated upon re-entry into the Earth's atmosphere? Where and how would it land? And how would it slow down?

Moments later, Earth was in sight in all its wonder and beauty. The temperature inside the box was increasing but remained tolerable even though the red glow around them as they made re-entry was increasing. Suddenly Tindorella flew forward and positioned herself directly in front of the box so that she was sustaining the full force and heat of re-entry. She was quite capable of an ordeal such as this and seemed to be enjoying herself as the almost comical movement of her huge wings testified. Tindorella was transformed into a bright red giant butterfly, and she looked both menacing and beautiful as they progressed through the Earth's atmosphere at a blistering pace. Tindorella's protective influence ensured that the transportation box was kept relatively cool and that the crew were comfortable as they hurtled through the air. What they could see as they peered through the tree roots and branches, was the red glow that was Tindorella.

After thirty minutes of re-entry, Tindorella's bright red glow began to fade, and they began to slow down. The decrease in speed was felt inside the ship as the force of gravity caused quite a few of the crew to lose their balance and to bump into the ship's infrastructure. After a further period of slowing down Tindorella released herself from the front of the box and she was again flying alongside them. The personnel on the flight deck now had a clear view of the Earth and the obvious question presented itself, where and how were they going to land and would they land safely?

Tindorella flew on ahead of them at some distance and the rectangular box followed her. The  very white lights of the four yew trees had now come together and formed one central beam that was focused on Tindorella's back, revealing her beautiful colours. They were losing altitude rapidly and Tindorella's flight path was erratic, swaying from side to side and dipping and diving at impossible angles but the beam from the yew trees never left her back. This, as you can imagine, produced a very uncomfortable experience for the occupants on board the ship who had once again been ordered to strap in and brace themselves.

Tindorella was surveying the territory below and was trying to find a particular landmark that she had identified from many previous flybys, long ago in the distant past. She was at an altitude of about five miles and was shifting at some speed when suddenly she spotted it. Flying to one side, she allowed the powerful beam of light from the yew trees to centre and focus on a strange architectural feature way below them. It was in fact a large Jacobean house, laid out in an E shape, with outer wings and a central courtyard. An imposing structure. It was made of stone from Caen in France and marble from Cararra in Italy. The beam of light lit up these features impressively but of much more importance to Tindorella and of much greater benefit for the butterfly population at large, were the extensive grounds and gardens that surrounded the house (the house was Hatfield House in Hertfordshire in England). They consisted of orchards, water fountains and water terraces but crucially, there were plenty of scented plants and herb gardens. The yew beam was focused on one particular area and this was to be their landed site, or runway. It was a rather intricate foot maze, bordered on either side by neat, well-manicured hedges and it was wide enough and not too complex, an ideal landing site in fact.

Tindorella was flying alongside once again, and the rectangular box was now swerving from side to side with the beam fully centred on the foot maze. As they descended, they soared through white puffy clouds, cumulus, cumonimbus and stunning blue skies and then there it was directly in front of them, the foot maze was about three miles away. Tindorella flew ahead and directed the vessel toward it. When they were within two miles of the maze, she flew upwards and away and landed on the other side, disappearing into the orchards and terraces. The box containing Sunjammer positioned itself and prepared to enter the maze. It was at the entrance in no time and locked onto the hedges on either side, carefully gliding its way along the contours, swerving and turning as it progressed along the maze. Eventually it reached the exit and passed through it, to be greeted by a vast, very well-manicured garden populated by fountains and formal pathways and all of this bordered by huge, deciduous leafy trees, scented plants and herb gardens. The rectangular container had come to a standstill and was hovering about six feet from the ground, very much like a hovercraft. Its power surge was creating a wind blast in all directions, disturbing the general flora and fauna but this had the effect of increasing the wonderful scents emanating from the varied flowers which was in turn exciting the crew of Sunjammer. The box finally settled on the ground, and all was very silent and still.

It then opened up completely, the cover comprising the tree roots and branches disintegrated into thin air and the large area of grass that had encased the crew for their journey back to Earth unfurled itself completely and blended in with the country park at Hatfield. The four yew trees had by now lost their bright lights, had served their purpose and were lost among the great many yew trees existing here.

Sunjammer now stood alone in this large country park.

Groundhog spoke "Fellow travellers, heroes and worthy comrades, we have arrived home. Please release yourselves from your harnesses. I have opened all doors, hatches and windows, please hover outside, escape from the ship and survey your beautiful surroundings. There is more than enough nectar, food and there are plenty of buddleia bushes for everyone." A mad scramble ensued as butterflies galore flew to the nearest exits and flew out, promptly landing on their own particular favourite flowers as they surveyed the lush environment.

The Tortoiseshells discovered their favourites, and the Burgundians found a superb giant oak tree dappled in sunlight, enabling them to spread their wings and absorb the heat. The Orange Tips discovered a vast deep purple coloured buddleia bush with a view to mating and laying their eggs on the undersides of a clump of stinging nettle leaves nearby.

Groundhog and Shunter made certain that every crew member had left the ship before they themselves departed and fluttered away, landing onto a large water fountain moulded as an Elizabethan courtier. Moments later, Sunjammer, their trusted and most reliable spaceship which had taken them on so many adventures was no more. Everybody stopped what they were doing and stared, stunned at this moment in time as Sunjammer began shaking violently as if in a temper. She began to sway very gently on the spot, with the breeze as if dancing but she was disintegrating. The acorn cups, sunflowers and butterfly wings that made up the spacecraft detached themselves and floated, gliding in all directions before disappearing among the tall Oaks, Elms, Ash, Yew and Scottish Pines.

(The Sunflowers would in fact find new homes and breeding grounds at Hatfield Park and would tell their children and grandchildren about their heroic adventures as part of the spaceship)

The bamboo canes which had formed Sunjammers skeletal framework launched themselves high into the sky, not unlike an army of archers releasing an array of arrows and landed over a wide area, (these heroic bamboo canes would provide a welcome support for wild peas and tomato plants to climb up). Finally, the super strong cobwebs that had been strung by the spiders in the construction of Sunjammer and which had been so very important for the success of the mission, floated with the wind to all four corners of Hatfield Park.

(These would prove invaluable in providing protection for bee colonies desperate for a haven  to stay away from envious predators)

She was gone. It was as though she had never existed. Everybody who witnessed this was amazed but there was also a deep sense of loss that Sunjammer would never be seen again but it didn't stop a huge round of applause and noise as butterfly wings clapped together to thank Sunjammer. A chapter had now closed but there was still one, rather large and important presence to be accounted for. Whilst the crew had been celebrating and reflecting on their successful mission and feeding on and exploring their new environment, they had failed to notice that at the very far end of Hatfield Park something unusual was occurring. Whilst they were surrounded by clear blue sky, at the other end of the park, the sky had turned a curious shade of crimson or deep red with blue streaks running through it. If you looked closely, you could see the vast canopy of trees blowing and swaying in unison. They were being disturbed by something when suddenly there was a high-pitched moan which drew the attention of the butterflies at the other end of the park. Emerging from behind the trees and slowly elevating into the sky was the majestic looking Tindorella. Her appearance had changed into that of a gladiatorial butterfly and her wings were constantly changing from scarlet to black, to blue and back to scarlet. Her torso was a constant hornet yellow, and her wing trimmings were a constant light blue.

"You, all of you, who successfully completed this mission to rescue me and restored me to health and vitality, please come forward into my presence where I can see you" announced Tindorella.

There was movement throughout Hatfield Park as the entire crew emerged from hedgerows and gardens and neatly aligned themselves in front of Tindorella. All were present and correct and Tindorella spoke.

"As a token of my deep appreciation and to honour you for what you have achieved, I have decided to reward you all with the highest honour known to the butterfly brotherhood. I will grant you total freedom of the vast cosmos, all the quadrants of the Nimbellum and the whole of the known universe, from the planet Earth to the Vesuvian Plains and beyond. To equip you in your obvious quest for adventure and exploration I am going to embolden and strengthen you with a durable and super strong casing which will allow you to conquer all potential adversaries. If I can ask you all to form a tight, compact circle, I will put this power into operation"

The heroic forty fluttered around in an excited state for a moment before forming a tight circle as Tindorella had requested. Tindorella then proceeded to hover directly over them as the trees, bushes and all the other surrounding vegetation swayed with the gust that she produced as she flew over. Even the still ponds in the ornamental gardens produced ripples across their surface.

After a while, everything became very still and very silent. Tindorella was motionless for a time but then her giant wings began to move, flapping very slowly and gently. They then began secreting a very fine silver substance laced with black tendrils. The substance hung in the air for a while before forming into an even thicker substance that eventually took the form of a silver cloud laced with black threading. It hovered between Tindorella and the butterfly group for a moment before falling and completely engulfing the group on the ground. There was no movement at all for a while but then the cloud began to disperse. It didn't disperse up into the sky as you would expect. It had absorbed itself into each and every crew member. They were unaware of it at first but each of them had been empowered with great strength and durability, their minds had also become very strong, and their actual physical appearance had changed so that they all looked the same. They were blue, black in colour but with a silver trim around the wing edges giving them all a very striking, handsome appearance. Their heads were black but laced with bright, silver specks.

Tindorella spoke again,'"Arise, dear saviours, you are now invincible. You will survey and protect the cosmos unhindered. All potential enemies will fall before you. I shall name you guardians of the cosmos and please know that you will always have a special place in my heart and in my soul".

With these final words, Tindorella started to move and gain height. Once again, the trees and all surrounding vegetation swayed furiously as she ascended, flapping her giant wings. She lurched to the left, shouted "Farewell, I am forever in your debt" and flew at great speed into the blue sky and was gone. The forty watched as she flew out of sight. They looked at each other and were indeed identical to each other. Groundhog had remembered Tindorella's words, strength, invincible and guardians of the cosmos.

"Firefly, Shunter, please escort me on a short flight around the park and gardens, will you?" said Groundhog.

The three of them ascended and to their amazement, they were flying at supersonic speed, weaving and diving above the lush, green canopy. Any obstacles were sliced apart without them knowing and everything was swaying furiously as they passed. Their minds had been forged together which allowed them to make decisions collectively and their concentration levels were bordering on 100% mindfulness with meditation. They hadn't needed to fly back to get the others because their superb meditative powers enabled them to communicate with them where they were, and they were almost immediately all joined together in a group again. The whole group were now flying through Hatfield Park, fluttering away and very happy with themselves and their newly acquired super-powers.

As newly promoted Guardians of the Cosmos, they needed to find a secure, fortress like headquarters and to this end Groundhog sent a telepathic message to everyone, informing them of his intentions and of the need to leave Hatfield House immediately, (nobody wanted to because the grounds were so beautiful and catered for their every need, including that of laying eggs and raising families) in order to find a safe, secure central headquarters from which to police the cosmos.

Our heroes had completed their mission and been duly rewarded. Part two of their greatest adventure had only just begun.

**THE END**

www.ingramcontent.com/pod-product-compliance
Lightning Source LLC
Chambersburg PA
CBRC092145180726
48295CB00007B/112